NY TIMES BESTSELLING AUTHOR

LYNN RAYE
HARRIS

HOT SEAL RESCUE

HOT SEAL TEAM

This is a work of fiction. Names, characters, places, brands, media, and incidents are either the product of the author's imagination or are used fictitiously. The author acknowledges the trademarked status and trademark owners of various products referenced in this work of fiction, which have been used without permission. The publication/use of these trademarks is not authorized, associated with, or sponsored by the trademark owners.

Interior Design by JT Formatting

www.**lynnrayeharris**.com

First Edition: September 2016
Library of Congress Cataloging-in-Publication Data

Harris, Lynn Raye
Hot SEAL Rescue / Lynn Raye Harris – 1st ed
ISBN-13: 978-1-941002-24-7

1. Hot SEAL Rescue —Fiction
2. Fiction—Romance
3. Fiction—Contemporary Romance

OTHER BOOKS BY LYNN RAYE HARRIS

HOSTILE OPERATIONS Team Series

Hot Pursuit (#1) – Matt & Evie

Hot Mess (#2) – Sam & Georgie

Hot Package (#3) – Billy & Olivia

Dangerously Hot (#4) – Kev & Lucky

Hot Shot (#5) – Jack & Gina

Hot Rebel (#6) – Nick & Victoria

Hot Ice (#7) – Garrett & Grace

Hot & Bothered (#8) – Ryan & Emily

Hot Protector (#9) – Chase & Sophie

HOT SEAL Team Series

HOT SEAL (#1) – Dane & Ivy

HOT SEAL Lover (#2) – Remy & Christina

CHAPTER ONE

"SWEETIE, THERE YOU are! Thank God!"

Cody "Cowboy" McCormick watched the woman approaching him in the lobby of the Venetian with an appreciative eye. She was utterly gorgeous, the kind of woman who made heads turn as she strode along on a pair of pencil-thin stilettos that looked positively painful. There were a lot of gorgeous women in Vegas, but this one had that extra something that drew the eye like a magnet.

He turned his head, looking for the lucky guy she was about to put her hands on—and maybe her lips. He didn't see a smiling dude anywhere. When Cody turned back to her, she was nearly upon him.

And then she was by his side, reaching for his arm, her flowery scent stealing into his nostrils and making him almost giddy with the sweetness of it as her fingertips brushed his bicep.

"Baby, my goodness, I thought you'd never arrive," she purred, winding her arm through his and wedging herself against his side, her smile bright and mesmerizing.

Luscious red lips. Cascading blond hair. Long fucking legs even though he calculated that without the heels she was probably around five foot five or so. Bright, almost golden, eyes stared back at him.

Too bad she was a loon, because she sure was mighty appetizing.

He opened his mouth to tell her she had the wrong guy, but her fingers tightened on his arm—and that's when he felt the hard, round cylinder pressed into his side. He let his gaze drop. Her hand was in her tiny purse, and that purse was jammed against him, the gun barrel unmistakable as it dug into his side.

His first instinct was to disarm her. He could take her down easily, but not without doing serious damage to the bones in her arm. Still, she was threatening him—and pretty as she was, that wasn't going to fly.

But there was something in her eyes, some look that said *I'm not crazy, honest. Help me.*

He lifted his gaze then and scanned the lobby area. There was a stocky man staring hard in their direction. He had three men with him, big and dressed in the quintessential suit of the professional bodyguard, while he wore what was clearly a custom pin-striped suit and chunky gold jewelry. He looked like a typical Vegas big shot—or a big shot wannabe.

Cody didn't like the man on principle. He looked down at the woman beside him again. Her lips were parted, her lipstick shiny and begging to be messed up.

But was she really trying to get away from these men, or playing him for a mark on someone's orders?

He didn't know, and he didn't have long to decide.

But he could play her game for a little bit. See what she was up to. Decide whether to disarm her and send the others packing or rescue her from harm.

"How about a kiss, sugar?" he drawled. "I've missed you."

Her eyes narrowed. "Let's get into the car first, all right?"

She shoved the pistol into his side even more. She deliberately didn't look back at the three hired goons who'd now started moving toward them. But he knew she sensed them coming because of the way her mouth hardened into a flat line. Was that a hint of desperation flaring in her eyes?

"Take me to your car, honey. Now."

"Sure thing, sugar." He'd made his decision. Whatever was happening here, she was not working with those men. He put his arm around her shoulders. She tensed, but she didn't shrug him off. They strolled toward the entrance and then out into the hot Vegas air, though it was nearly sunset now and things were cooling off.

The traffic in front of the hotel was jammed with cars and taxis. Picking up, dropping off, waiting. He didn't know where she thought they were going, but getting anywhere fast on the Vegas Strip was impossible. The taxi line was packed with people, but he walked up to the bellman and handed him a twenty.

"Need a taxi. *Now.*"

The man took one look at the woman hanging on Cody's arm and then grinned as he pocketed the money. "You bet, man."

The bellman signaled for a taxi, and one careened up to the curb. He opened the door, and Cody and the woman got inside while people in the taxi line grumbled. The door slammed.

"Where to?" the taxi driver asked.

Cody lifted an eyebrow as he studied the woman. "Well?"

She still had the gun pressed into his side. She took a deep breath, her breasts swelling against the tight red material of her wrap dress. "Where are you staying?"

"The Rio." It wasn't the best casino in Vegas, but it was cheaper than those on the Strip. Plus his cousin worked there, so Cody got a great rate whenever he was in town.

"Then that's where we're going. The Rio."

"The Rio," the taxi driver said. "Got it."

"And hurry," the woman said. "There's a fifty in it for you if you get us out of here in the next two seconds."

Just then the men from the hotel burst onto the portico, and the driver jammed the gas. Cody didn't know how the man did it, but he found a slot in the traffic and shoved his way through without scraping metal. Somehow they were rolling toward the street.

Cody reached up and slid the glass partition closed so he could talk to the woman without the driver listening in. "Care to tell me your name?"

She eased back against the seat, her purse still pointing at him. Her eyes sparked. The creamy swells of her breasts rose and fell as she breathed. It was distracting. She had a small waist beneath those amazing tits. He wondered if they were fake but decided they weren't when the taxi bumped over the curb as it turned onto the street and her flesh jiggled.

"Call me Jane," she finally said.

"Well, Jane, do you plan to tell me what's going on?"

"No."

At least she was honest. He turned and looked behind them, but there didn't appear to be any signs of pursuit. Not that anyone could pursue easily in this traffic. Unlike in the movies, it would be a slow car chase where drivers honked and cussed and traffic lights lasted for what seemed like hours.

"So what happens next?"

She glanced behind them, the tension in her body not easing one bit. "We go to the Rio. You get out and go your way. I'll go mine."

"Aren't you considerate? Planning to drop me off after kidnapping me in broad daylight."

"It was necessary."

"Why'd you pick me? There were half a dozen men standing around in there."

Her lips tightened, and then she shrugged. "You were alone. You're big and kind of tough-looking—and you were staring at me like you'd like to get into my panties. I needed a way out, and you were there."

Yeah, perhaps he had been staring. A man would have to be dead not to want into those panties. But he figured he wasn't the only one who'd been looking. Still, she'd chosen him out of all of them.

"Didn't it worry you that I might not cooperate?"

She snorted. "Not especially. I can be persuasive when I need to be."

"The pistol, you mean."

"It gets the job done."

"Is it real?"

She blinked. "What? Of course it's real."

He shrugged. “They make lighters that look like guns. Probably feel remarkably the same when concealed in a purse.”

“It’s a Sig P239. Guaranteed to put a hole in you, sweet cheeks. Don’t try me.”

Cody’s interest took a giant leap. Sig Sauer P239s were used in spec ops. Semiautomatic, 9mm. Small enough to be concealed in an evening purse—but wicked enough to blow holes in anything that got in the way. His official weapon was in a locker back at the base, unfortunately. His personal ones were in his house. Not one of them where they would do him any good.

If he’d driven to Vegas instead of flying, he’d have been armed. As it was, he had nothing but skill and training to get him out of this situation.

Not that he was worried about it. Still easy to disarm her, though she’d turned her body against the door and faced him across the rear seat, her hand still inside the purse.

“So you’d shoot me in front of a witness?” He tsked. “Not too bright, is it?”

Her golden eyes were flat. “I’d have to shoot him too. So don’t make that happen, all right?”

CHAPTER TWO

MIRANDA LOCKWOOD'S HEART thumped even as she tried to concentrate on slowing it down. She'd learned some breathing techniques, a few thought experiments—and they usually worked whenever she did them. The aim was to center her focus and make her ready for whatever assignment she'd been given.

This one— God, this one was a clusterfuck. How had Victor Conti known she wasn't what she'd claimed to be? She'd spent months studying him, months planning this mission—and her cover'd been blown within days. The only saving grace was that he'd been so certain of his ability to punish her that he'd revealed the information too soon.

If he'd waited until they'd been somewhere more private— Well, she wouldn't be here now. Wouldn't be in this tiny taxi with this infuriatingly calm and seriously sexy man.

That chiseled jaw— Heavens, she didn't think they

really made those anywhere but Hollywood. But Henry Cavill had nothing on this guy.

Miranda drew in a deep breath and told herself to concentrate. She had to get out of this mess. She had to ditch this guy, find a car, and make contact with her handler. Then she had to get out of Vegas before Conti's people found her.

Jesus, what had she gotten herself into?

"You look troubled, Jane."

She almost didn't respond, but then she'd told this guy her name was Jane, hadn't she? She didn't know why she'd done it considering it was her actual middle name. Her cover name was Tiffany White, and she'd spent a long time getting accustomed to answering to that. Months, goddammit.

And now it was over. She hadn't stopped Conti from doing anything. Hadn't found out where the hub of his business was or where he was shipping the guns and drugs. She also hadn't found out a thing about Mark. Hell, she'd promised she would find Mark's killer, but she still hadn't managed it.

Four years in the CIA, eight months since Mark's death, and she still didn't know a damned thing. All she knew was that she missed him. He'd been her mentor, her lover at one time, and her friend.

And now he was gone, his life snuffed out in a single moment by someone in Conti's organization. She was *certain* she was on the right track. But holy fuck, now what?

"Jane?"

She snapped her gaze to Mister Tall, Dark, and Sexy. He had coal-black hair, blue eyes, and tanned skin that said he'd spent time in the sun. His chest was broad beneath his white button-down. He wore faded jeans and cowboy boots, and her tongue nearly tripped over itself as her eyes made the journey from those boots back up to firm, kissable lips.

Well hell, since when had her libido decided to return? She'd been with no one in over a year. To feel the stirring of desire now was inconvenient—and definitely not happening, no matter how sexy this guy was.

And hey, just because he was big and brawny didn't mean his dick matched the exterior package. What a disappointment that would be. Not to mention, though he looked tough, he most likely wasn't. A gym rat who appealed to the ladies because of his physique, but put him in a do-or-die situation and this pretty boy was going to die more likely than not.

"Yeah, cowboy?" she tossed out with more than a hint of contempt.

His brows drew together for a second, and she wondered if she'd insulted him. Then she shrugged mentally. Who cared if she had? She wasn't going to see him ever again. In about ten minutes, they were parting ways forever.

"I'm not a danger to you," he said. "You don't have to grip that gun so tightly. Relax a minute, breathe while you can. Those guys aren't far behind, but they're far enough."

She sucked in a breath. How would he know? "Doesn't matter how far they are. They know who I am now."

Jeez, had she really just said that? She was slipping. *Dammit, Mark, why did you trust me in the first place?*

"And who are you, Jane?"

There was an ache in her chest. A knot in the pit of her stomach. Who was she? Hell, she'd like to know that herself. She'd never really known. She just reinvented herself for whatever job came along and then pretended it didn't matter.

But that wasn't what he was asking. He was asking for her name, the name those bastards now knew. How had that happened? The moment she got Badger on the phone, she was going to find out what the ever-loving fuckity-fuck had gone wrong back there.

"Nobody important. Just a girl with bad judgement."

The taxi pulled into the circular driveway of the Rio, and Miranda thought about what would happen next. She'd head into the casino, make her way through to the parking garage, and then she'd borrow a ride.

Basic but effective. Keep changing the dynamic. Confuse the bastards until she could get to the safe house. She just prayed the safe house wasn't compromised. Considering how badly this day was going, nothing would surprise her.

"Go around to the side," she ordered. "The bus loading zone."

The driver shrugged. "Your money."

But he did as he was told. She glared at the big dude she'd abducted when the taxi came to a stop. "Don't forget the extra fifty," she told him when he dipped into his wallet.

He glanced up at her as he took the bills and thrust them through the window. Another second and they were out on the street. She searched the surrounding area, looking for any signs of Conti and his men.

She spun and started walking toward the casino.

"Hey."

She glanced up at Mister Tall, Dark, and Sexy. He kept pace with her, striding through the doors of the casino and into the smoky hell it contained.

"You can go now, cowboy. Thanks for giving me some cover."

"I think you're in trouble, Jane. I think you could use some backup."

She stopped and a cocktail waitress deftly spun around her before they collided. The casino wasn't crowded yet, but it was getting there. The smoke permeated the air in spite of the filters that sucked it out, and the bells and whistles of the slots rang with abandon. Scantily clad women carried trays of drinks between slots, and people hunched over machines, cigarettes dangling from mouths while they kept pressing the button to bet again.

"And what makes you think you're qualified to provide backup?" No way in hell was she accepting the help of a guy she didn't know, but he intrigued her more than he should. Too pretty by half.

Time's wasting, girlie.

"The name's Cody, by the way."

"Cody. Fine. Look, I don't have time for small talk, and I'm not going to sleep with you. You can run along now. Go find a waitress to fuck or something, but stop wasting my time."

He took a step into her before she knew what he was about. Instinctively, she stepped back on her heel and prepared to attack.

His hands moved like lightning. A moment later, she was staring at her purse tucked under his arm. *Holy shit.*

"Give me that back. Now."

He looked too cool for words. Unfazed. She was having to revise her opinion of him, and she didn't like what this new development said about what she'd thought of him in the first place. Was she losing her touch?

"Not happening, Jane. Not until you tell me who you are and what's going on."

CHAPTER THREE

JANE STARED AT him with wide eyes. And then her mouth hardened and her chest swelled as she sucked in air. "I need that back, asshole. Don't make me take it away from you."

Cody nearly laughed. "Take it away from me? Sure, you can try."

"Are you purposely trying to get me killed, or do you just not understand plain English?" Her voice was strained, but not from the effort of trying to be heard in the noisy casino.

"I'm a SEAL, Jane. I can help. Tell me what you need."

She looked like she might kick him in the balls, but then her chin lifted. "I need a car. I need to get the fuck out of Vegas as quickly as possible."

"You're in luck. I have a car."

"Why should I care? Give me back my purse and I'll find my own car, thanks."

He snorted. "You'd seriously steal a car when you could just let me drive you?"

"I don't know you. I don't trust you."

He started toward the elevators, certain she would follow. He wasn't wrong. She kept pace with him in those killer stilettos, but only because he wasn't trying to get away from her.

"Where are you going?"

"To my room. I need to get my stuff."

"Look, asshole, just give me back my purse and forget you ever met me. It's safer for you."

"Apparently you didn't hear me. I'm a SEAL, honey. I don't walk away from a challenge."

He stepped into the elevator as it opened and then turned to see what she would do. Her mouth was tight as she passed inside the shiny interior. She went to the wall opposite and then turned to face him, leaning back against the railing in such a way that her chest was exaggerated. He couldn't figure out if she was trying to distract him or not. Still, he kept his eyes firmly fixed to her face as the doors slid closed and the noise of the casino faded.

"What are you doing in Vegas, sailor? Shore leave?"

"Something like that."

She snorted. "Who's hiding something now?"

Hiding something? Yeah, he was, though it surprised him she'd deduced that much from the few words he'd said.

But he always hid his feelings when it came to his mother. He thought of the call he'd gotten from his grandfather a few days ago, telling him that his mother was drinking again. And when Maggie was drinking, she was hitting the casinos. Doing recreational drugs, sleeping with random guys, searching for her newest sugar daddy. Whatever it took to get high and ease the pain of her many demons.

Cody's jaw tightened. Fucking demons. He'd never really known what they were, but he was pretty sure he was the result of one of them. She'd had him far too young, left him with her parents, and only came home on occasion to see him. When she was home and clean, she was his mother to the best of her ability in spite of the fact he often felt more mature than she was. When she fell off the wagon, she was self-destructive.

He hadn't found her yet, but that's because she didn't want to be found. And, frankly, he was tired of dragging her out of messes of her own making. She was on a bender, but she'd return in a week or two, repentant and promising this was the last time.

It never was the last time. If not for his aging grandparents, he'd probably leave her to her own devices because he was fucking sick of the emotional manipulation. It worked on her parents and she knew it. Thrived on it.

It did not work on him.

If he hadn't already been planning a trip back, he wouldn't have made a special one. But one of his teammates was getting married in Vegas next week, and Cody had tacked on some vacation time to see his grandparents first since they lived a few hours away.

"Not hiding anything that could get me killed, darlin'. Promise you that."

The elevator doors opened then and he exited, heading for his room. He deliberately turned his back on Jane, though he was certain she knew a thing or two about self-defense. He wasn't worried she'd get the jump on him here. For one thing, she was too far behind, scuttling along on those heels and trying to catch up now that he'd lengthened his stride.

When he reached his door, he turned to watch her. Her face was a thundercloud and he chuckled to himself. Yeah, she'd been planning to try to disarm him, but she'd been unable to catch him.

He unlocked the door and went into the room. It was a big room by your typical hotel standards, with a king-sized bed, a couch, two chairs, a desk, and an armoire with a TV. Either his cousin had hooked him up or all the rooms were this big. It definitely wasn't a high-class hotel, but it wasn't dilapidated either.

Jane tottered in and sank onto the couch, pulling off her shoes and rubbing her feet. "Jesus these things are torture."

"So why the fuck are you wearing them?" he asked as he grabbed his things and stuffed them into his duffel.

"Because it was necessary."

"Don't suppose you have a change of clothes in this thing?" he asked, holding up the purse he'd kept tucked under his arm.

"Unfortunately, no. My clothes are at the Venetian."

"Anything identifying? Any clues to where you might go from there?"

She shook her head. "Definitely not."

He narrowed his eyes at her. "So which is it? FBI? DEA?"

He didn't miss the tightening of her features. Bingo. He'd hit on the fact she was employed by the US government, and she didn't like it.

"Neither."

"Where's your phone? Shouldn't you have a way to be in contact?"

She looked a little pained. "No phones allowed around Victor Conti. His men would confiscate it if I dared. So no, I don't have one."

"You use burners, am I right? Probably have the numbers you need memorized."

She inclined her head, giving him that much. Her whiskey eyes sparked with heat and intelligence.

"What I don't understand is this—where's your back-up? And how did you think you were getting a gun through that guy's security when you wouldn't take a phone with you?"

She tugged at the skirt of her dress. A gesture of dis-comfort. "First of all, this isn't the movies, cowboy. We don't all work with secretive teams backing us up, hunker-ing over computer screens in hotel rooms and listening to everything we say. Some ops are more basic."

"So this is an op."

She looked frustrated. "That's none of your busi-ness."

"You made it my business when you shoved a pistol in my ribs—and you still haven't explained how you ex-pected to get by with carrying a gun."

"I didn't expect to get by with it. I expected them to confiscate it—but I wanted them to know that I carry a weapon and know how to use it. Assholes like that don't respect anything less. Besides, there's no incriminating information they can get off a gun—at least not off that gun. If I took a phone and they forced me to unlock it? No way." She raked a hand through her hair and swore. "Why the hell didn't I choose the nerd?"

He blinked. "What?"

"The tall, skinny guy with glasses and suspenders standing four feet to your left."

Cody remembered the guy. He'd been standing next to the sculpture in the atrium, gazing up at it in rapt attention. Then he'd seen good old Jane here striding over, and his jaw had hit the floor. He'd ceased staring at the sculpture and started staring at her. If she'd walked up to him, he'd have pissed himself.

"You didn't choose him because he would have gotten you caught. Probably faint at the hint you had a weapon, or scream, and then what?"

"Yes, then what?" She sighed, and he finished tossing his stuff in the bag. Then he took his phone out of his pocket and hit a button.

"Yo, Cowboy, whassup?" It was Remy Marchand's voice on the other end of the line. His SEAL team's second-in-command—and the guy getting married in a few days.

Cody eyed the gorgeous Jane sitting on his couch. She looked wary but resigned. "Got a situation, Cage. Might need some backup."

CHAPTER FOUR

MIRANDA DIDN'T LIKE that he was sharing what had happened so far with someone on the phone, but there wasn't any way to stop him. She eyed him as he talked, her blood humming with interest and frustration combined.

It was the kind of frustration that came from being stuck here with a man who'd gotten the jump on her, not sexual frustration.

Though, dammit, there was a particular buzzing in the vicinity of her nether regions that indicated parts of her might be interested in parts of him if the timing was right.

Why oh why couldn't she be a normal woman on a trip to Vegas? Maybe one who'd gotten dumped and had come here to ease her broken heart? A little hot sex with a handsome stranger might just be the way to cure that kind of pain, though Miranda wouldn't know.

She'd never been dumped, and she'd never spent enough time with any one guy to get hung up on him. Mark had been different. He'd saved her from God only knows what kind of life when he'd plucked her from a strip club at the tender age of eighteen. He'd been part of a joint task force sting operation to bring down a drug network that had been centered in the club. She'd been so new there, so green, just trying to find her way in a world that had never been very welcoming.

It's what happened when you ran away from home and didn't have any plan for how to take care of yourself.

Mark had done a lot for her, though she'd hardly seen him for two years after that night. When she was twenty-two, she'd joined the CIA. When she was twenty-three, he'd finally come to see her as adult enough to make her own decisions about sleeping with him.

The sex was comfortable, not earth-shattering, but that's what she wanted. Comfort.

There was nothing comfortable about the throbbing need manifesting inside her nether regions right now. No, this kind of desire was not something rational or sensible.

Cody the Cowboy—she thought of him that way because of the boots and faded jeans, though why that was she couldn't say—still had her purse under his arm. It was funny in a way, and not so funny in all the ways that mattered.

Holy shit but he'd disarmed her fast. Before she even knew he intended it. Yeah, that made her angry because it knocked her off her game. Was she getting so bad that she couldn't defend against such a maneuver? Hell, she hadn't even seen it coming—and that was embarrassing in the extreme.

What would Badger say? What would Mark have said? They'd be ashamed of her, she was certain.

She took comfort in the fact that as quickly as he'd

disarmed her, he could have killed her if that was his intention. If he'd been working for Conti, he'd have done it already.

Unless Conti wanted to find out who else was involved in this operation…

Miranda shook her head. No, that wasn't his style at all. Besides, he already knew something because he'd known who she was. Her cover had been blown, and that wasn't easy to do. She had to consider the implications of that—an inside job?

Possibly.

"Yo, Jane—care to provide any further information for my buddies here?" Cody was standing over her with the phone at his ear. Waiting for her to say who she was and what she was doing.

Not happening.

"Sorry, no. I could tell you, but then I'd have to kill you."

Cody snorted. "See, man?" he said into the phone. "Told you it wasn't happening. … Yeah, all right. Call you in two hours."

He ended the call and slipped the phone into his jeans. Then he opened up her purse, removed the Sig, cleared it—and ejected the clip. Son of a bitch.

He gave her a shit-eating grin that made her want to clock him as he tossed the gun and purse back to her.

"What the fuck am I supposed to do with this?" she demanded, holding up the empty Sig.

"Dunno, baby. But until you tell me who you are and what this is all about, I'm not giving you the ammo."

Miranda got to her feet. "And just how do you expect me to defend myself?"

His grin didn't change. "I'm sure you'll think of something." He shouldered his duffel bag. "Come on, let's get out of here."

Miranda grabbed her shoes. No way was she putting them on just yet. "Wait a minute—just where do you think we're going anyway? You have no idea who I am, or where I need to go, or even who's after me—"

"Now that's where you're wrong, sunshine. I do know who's after you. You told me his name, remember?"

Miranda barely refrained from rolling her eyes. Literal-ass jerk. "He's dangerous. You have no idea."

"Sure I do. I just found out all I needed to know about Victor Conti. He deals in drugs and guns for the most part with some petty sex trade on the side. Porn films typically, mostly because he likes to watch the filming—oh, and then he likes to take the starlets home and reenact the whole thing privately."

Miranda could only gape. It had taken weeks of work to gather all that information. So far as she knew, it was classified. And yet this cowboy knew it all in a matter of minutes.

"You aren't a Navy SEAL," she said, her heart thumping. "I don't know who you are, but you aren't that."

"Actually, I am. But I work for an organization that, uh, knows things. If you're involved with Conti, then you're either with the FBI, DEA, or the CIA. Conti's illegal activities fall under the areas of interest for any of the three."

Crap.

"So care to tell me which one it is?" he finished. "Might make this a bit easier for both of us."

"You planning to give me back my ammunition if I

do?"

"Depends," he said.

Miranda sighed. Her default setting was not to trust anyone, but maybe she needed to start. Not that she'd tell him everything. Definitely not. But she could give him enough to relax his guard—and then she could give him the slip when she got the chance.

Or, hell, maybe he'd prove to be useful after all.

"CIA," she said. "We're interested in the arms dealing, of course. He's been supplying guns to ISIS and the Freedom Force, among others, for quite some time. But he's also putting assault weapons on the streets here, and that's not a good thing. Of course, that's the FBI's territory, but we're cooperating on this one."

"So what's your real name, Jane?"

"Actually, that is my real name—my middle name. My first name is Miranda."

"Miranda," he said softly, and a shiver ran down her spine. Liquid heat took up residence in her core, spilling out into her limbs. All because of the way he said her name. What the hell was that about?

"That's right. Can I have my clip back now?"

"Not quite. Give me a last name."

"Why do you need that?" It was against her religion to share her details. She'd had that drummed into her during the years of covert ops. Trust no one.

"Mine is McCormick. Cody McCormick, United States Navy. I work for an organization you've probably heard of, but I'm going to bet you thought it was a myth. Unless you've ever worked with us before, and then you know."

HOT. He had to be talking about the Hostile Operations Team, but she wasn't going to be the first to speak the name. Yeah, she knew about them. Mark had done ops with them before in the Middle East. She'd once spent a rough two days in the embassy in Baghdad with a group of HOT operators. They'd been there to extract a major who'd gotten nabbed in a market and taken prisoner. But then the embassy came under attack, and she'd thought for sure the major was dead.

He wasn't though. HOT came through.

"And what phantom group is this?" she replied, because she wasn't going to let on that she knew.

"We're called HOT. We deal in pretty much all the shit nobody else wants to. We go where none dare."

Where None Dare. Yes, she remembered that from the team she'd spent time with. They were proud of that.

For the first time, she felt a little bit of relief flowing through her. "My name is Miranda Lockwood. That's not the name Conti was supposed to know—but he does. I don't know how, but I've been compromised."

Saying the words aloud was like releasing the pressure in a valve. She felt as if a weight was gone even though nothing had been resolved.

Wordlessly, Cody handed her the clip to her weapon. She took it and slid it home. Then she put the gun into her purse and draped the chain over her shoulder. The sense of relief washing through her was strong. She was used to staying on her guard, and she still would, of course, but his gesture meant something. He wasn't out to kill her. At least not immediately.

"Thank you."

"You're welcome. Trust me now?"

She shrugged. "I don't trust anyone. But I believe

we're on the same side. At least for now."

"I'm going to help you, Miranda. We're getting out of here. Promise."

She'd love to believe him, but she'd learned never to count the chickens before the eggs hatched. That's how you ended up dead in this business.

"I'm going to need a change of clothes and a burner," she said, all businesslike. "Can you manage that?"

He shot her that sexy grin again. It melted through her like a flame cutting through wax. "Sunshine, I can manage anything you need."

CHAPTER FIVE

MIRANDA WAS AS jumpy as a cat in a room full of rocking chairs, as Cody's grandma always said. She fidgeted in her seat, swiveling her head to look out the rear window of his rented Explorer. He'd taken a chance returning her clip, but he'd felt like it was necessary to get her to trust him. So far, so good.

Cody navigated the big vehicle through the crowded streets of Las Vegas, heading south. He'd first thought about taking her home to his grandparents' place up north, but considering the kind of man Victor Conti was, that probably wasn't the best idea. Cody didn't know what Miranda was into, or what kind of hell she might call down on them once she made her call back to her handler.

Fortunately, Cage had called him with directions to a safe house in Arizona. "It's not much," he'd said. "But it'll be a good place to go while we figure things out on this end."

He hoped like hell they did figure it out. Someone

had betrayed her—that's what she said, and Cody tended to believe her. He didn't think she'd been careless with her information, but then again he didn't know anything about her as an operative. He'd gotten the jump on her, so why couldn't others?

So many questions about Miranda Jane Lockwood—and few answers.

"What about those clothes, cowboy?" Miranda said as they passed yet another shopping center.

He glanced at her. Funny how everyone in his life called him cowboy even if they didn't know he'd grown up on a ranch. He'd ridden in more than a few rodeos—bulls, broncs, and roping—but he didn't do a whole lot of that anymore, unless you counted mechanical bulls at honky-tonk bars. There just wasn't any time for it.

He rode horses when he was back home for a visit, and he worked the ranch even though his grandfather had enough hired help. After being on a dangerous mission, it was relaxing to spend hours in the saddle moving cattle from one pasture to another.

"Why do you call me cowboy?"

She shrugged and turned to look out the window again. Her profile was so pretty. Her lips pressed forward in a pout before she spoke, as if she was thinking.

"You're wearing boots that look broken in, rather than a shiny new pair, and faded jeans." She shrugged. "Stick a cowboy hat on you and there you go. You look like you could really live that life. Tourists always stand out, but you look like the real deal."

He laughed. "Fair enough, I guess. I grew up on a ranch, though the Navy is my home now."

"So the boots are authentic then."

"They are indeed. Been wearing them since I was about eighteen, I think. Nothing like a good pair of broken-in boots."

"About those clothes," she said.

He laid on the horn when some asshole in an exotic car cut him off. "I thought it was safer to get away from the city before stopping."

She didn't respond, and he knew she was fuming.

"How long you been an agent, Miranda Jane?"

Her head whipped around, two whiskey-colored eyes staring back at him. "Long enough. Too long maybe."

"Too long?" He glanced at her. "You don't look like you've been out of high school for very long."

"I'm twenty-six."

"Me too."

"So how long have you been a SEAL?"

"Five years. And don't think I didn't notice how you changed the subject just now."

He could tell she didn't want to do it, but she couldn't stop herself. One corner of her mouth turned up in a smile. "You're on to me."

He'd like to be on her all right. On her, in her, with her all the way to the end of an explosive orgasm. His dick started to throb with arousal, and he called up the most unattractive images he could think of to get it to stop.

"Yeah, well, don't change the subject," he said gruffly.

"I'm not telling you anything. I've already said too much, in fact."

"If I'd let you go back there, you wouldn't be any better off than you are right now. Conti has spies everywhere. Guarantee you he knows we went to the Rio by now. He probably knows the room we entered and when we left. He also knows we're in a rental, and he probably knows the plate number—"

"Which means we have to ditch this thing," she said very coolly.

He admired the way she didn't unravel under pressure. "Yes, ma'am, we do. I've got my guys working on getting us another car."

"You've thought of everything," she murmured.

"It's my job." It was, but he hadn't expected to be doing it for another few days. Visit the grandparents, try to find Maggie, go to Cage's wedding to Christina—the sister of the Alpha Squad commander, no less, and one seriously sexy lady, though saying that to Cage's face would get him pummeled—and then back to DC and whatever new assignment awaited.

Life as he expected it to be, even if the bit about going on missions and risking his life was unpredictable from one operation to the other.

"Good thing for me, I guess."

"Yes." He glanced at her. "Where's your backup? Why were you on this op alone?"

She didn't look at him. "I don't work with a team the way you do," she said. "Some things require a lot of preparation and delicacy."

"So if things went wrong, which they did, you had to get yourself out? Sounds like a shitty op to me."

"I don't question the work. I just do it."

It didn't make a lot of sense to him, but then he wasn't CIA. Still, she couldn't have been operating entirely alone—unless what she was doing was off the books. Now *that* was possible, sure. And it was mighty intriguing.

She let out a breath and turned to look at him. "I need to call my contact as soon as possible—which means I'd appreciate a burner and some clothing."

"I'm aware of that, sunshine. You've told me a couple of times now."

"Yes, but you don't seem to be doing anything about it."

Irritation was beginning to creep around the edges of his cool. "I'm telling you it's not safe yet. Or didn't they teach you anything in spy school?"

The corners of her mouth tightened. "You can't think of any alternatives? Like I'll hide in the backseat and you can go in without me?"

Cody snorted. "And come back outside to find you gone? No, thanks."

She only stared at him for a long moment. "Why do you even care? You don't know me. After this is over, you won't ever see me again. What's it matter what happens to me?"

He shot her a look. "It matters because my job is saving people from harm. I don't put them in the path of it and then walk away."

"I didn't ask you to save me. I'm capable of saving myself."

"Maybe so, sunshine—but I'm with you until we reach your people, so you might as well get used to it."

CHAPTER SIX

UNTIL THEY REACHED her people.

She wasn't sure who it was safe to reach out to anymore, quite honestly.

Miranda turned away and looked at the buildings beginning to slip by faster and faster as they eased out of central Las Vegas and its jammed traffic. There was a store for artificial lawns that made her do a double take. But yeah, if you couldn't afford to water a lawn out here—and how many people really could?—fake seemed to be the way to go if you wanted greenery.

Fake lawns. So foreign to her. She'd grown up in rural Alabama where the grass was greener than emeralds and the dirt was red clay. She shuddered as she thought about the dilapidated trailer where she'd lived with her parents and five sisters. Her father was a chain-smoking coal miner who worked long hours and then took out his anger on his wife and kids.

Her mother was an alcoholic who spent her days hiding the whiskey she drank and pretending she was fine when she really wasn't. Miranda had known how to shoot a gun by the time she was five. She'd learned how to cook by age six. She'd spent long days outside, wandering wherever she pleased while her mother lay in a stupor inside the dimly lit trailer with the anemic air conditioner turned up full blast. She and her sisters missed more school than they attended. If not for Mark, she'd have never gotten her GED or gone to college.

A wave of loneliness washed over her at the thought of Mark. She'd loved him. It had been a comfortable love born of familiarity and gratitude, not a deep, romantic love that ate her up from the inside out. He'd been her friend, the one person who knew what she came from and what she refused to go back to.

And now he was gone. His body had been unidentifiable, and for a long time she'd thought maybe he'd survived the bomb blast, maybe there'd been a mistake.

But Mark would have contacted her somehow. As the months went by and he didn't get in touch, she accepted what she'd known was true and gave up on irrational hope. Mark Reed was dead, killed on a mission to infiltrate Conti's operations and get to the heart of the organization.

Miranda leaned her head back and closed her eyes. Her heart hurt and she was tired. Cody wasn't stopping to get her new clothing anytime soon, and she had no way to call Badger just yet. It was two hours since she'd gone to meet with Conti, but Badger wouldn't be expecting contact for a while because he had no idea anything was wrong.

He'd warned her when he'd given her this assignment that she'd be alone for much of it, but she'd still jumped at the chance. And now it was over and she'd gotten nothing.

She didn't sleep, but she dozed in fits, snapping awake every few minutes or so it seemed. It was dark now, and the road had less traffic than it had earlier. She peered into the blackness. The lack of dwellings told her they were in the desert, and her belly twisted. What if this was all an elaborate setup? What if Cody the SEAL was really something else altogether?

It took her a moment to disabuse herself of that notion. The man was military, no doubt about it, and he'd said he was with HOT. Yeah, that could be a lie, but how would he have known that she'd ever even heard of HOT, let alone had personal experience with them?

He wouldn't—and still didn't know about the personal experience part.

"Where are we?" she asked.

"Almost to the drop point for this vehicle."

A few minutes later, he pulled into a gas station. He eased the Explorer over to where a Dodge Ram sat. "That's our ride," he said, putting the SUV into park and turning off the ignition.

Miranda looked longingly at the convenience store attached to the gas station. "I don't suppose you could go in there and get me a burner?"

"No need," Cody said, opening the door and climbing out. "Everything's in the Ram."

Miranda got out of the SUV. She'd put the heels back on since she had nothing else, but she hoped like hell there were some tennis shoes in that Ram. Cody got his bag and they went and climbed into the Dodge. It was a big four-door truck, gray, with comfortable seats and four-wheel drive. In the back seat, there was a shopping bag. Miranda rifled through it, grabbing the package with the phone first.

She glanced at Cody, hesitating. She didn't want to call Badger with him sitting right there, but what choice did she have?

She ripped the plastic packaging apart, powered up the phone, and plugged it into the battery backup that was also inside the bag. After she set the phone to block the number she was calling from, she dialed the number imprinted on her brain.

Badger picked up on the second ring. "Yes?"

"It's me."

"Mandy? How did it go? You okay?"

She blew out a breath and ran a hand through her hair, tossing the long blond strands over her shoulders. What she wouldn't give for a ponytail holder right about now.

"I'm okay. But the mission is a bust. He knew my identity."

There was silence on the other end of the phone. And then Badger swore long and hard. "Where are you? I'll send help."

Miranda glanced at Cody. He'd eased the truck onto the highway, but of course he was listening. "I have help."

"You do?" Badger sounded shocked.

"Yes. For now."

"You need to come in," he said, his voice sounding a little strained. "It's critical we get you into protection."

She knew it was, and yet there was something holding her back. Something not quite right about the entire situation. How had Conti known who she was? *How?*

Until she figured that out, she wasn't safe.

"I'm not ready to come in," she said, shocking herself and Badger too if the way he sucked in a breath was any indication. Until that moment, she hadn't really known she wouldn't obey protocol and go in.

"Mandy—"

"No. Listen. I've been compromised. The mission has been compromised. There's a leak. How else could he have found out who I was?"

"You're right," Badger said very quietly. "Of course you're right. I should have never sent you. We should have found another way."

Because they'd both wanted to find Mark's killer and bring him—or her—to justice.

"There wasn't another way. Besides, if I'd found the information we wanted, it would have been worth it."

"Yes, it would have."

She glanced at Cody. The light from the dash illuminated a strong, chiseled jaw and sculpted nose. How was it possible to look that good and not be a movie star?

"I'll call you again in a couple of hours."

"Tell me where you are at least. Still in Nevada?"

"'Bye, Badger." She clicked off the line before he could chastise her.

"Badger wasn't happy with you, I take it."

It wasn't a question. She tried not to be annoyed that Cody used Badger's name so casually, but then she'd said the name in his hearing. It didn't matter though, because Badger was a code name, not a real name. She knew Badger's real name. But that was irrelevant right now.

"Not really." She ran a hand over her head, tucking her hair behind her ears. "I don't think either one of us can quite believe I'm not going in."

"Something doesn't feel right or you would. Am I right?"

Miranda let out a shaky sigh and turned to look at his

profile. His ridiculously handsome profile. "Yes."

"Care to talk about it?"

She closed her eyes and wished she had a cigarette. But she'd given those up years ago. Sometimes she missed the nicotine filling her lungs and sending calming vapors throughout her body. Poisonous vapors, but still.

She shouldn't talk, and yet what did she have to lose? She no longer trusted the agency. She had no one to turn to. She was out in the cold, and it felt very, very odd. She just wanted to rewind the clock, have her meeting with Conti, and get the information she needed.

"He shouldn't have known who I was. This mission… it's off the books. Small scale, tightly controlled. Few people know anything about it."

"Then you need to decide which one of them betrayed you."

Her heart thumped. Yes, that was the only explanation. But why? Money?

Probably. Conti was wealthy, and this wouldn't be the first time he'd bought his way out of an investigation. Grease some palms, pay off an agent or two.

God, it was disgusting to think about.

"I don't know everyone involved. There's Badger, of course. A couple of others in the chain—beyond that, I don't know."

"Could it be personal? Or is it more that someone doesn't want Conti taken down?"

Miranda bit her lip. She'd been thinking about that—and the truth was she didn't know the answer.

"I wish I knew."

"Piss anyone off lately?"

Miranda snorted. "All the time. But trying to get me

killed for it is a bit extreme."

Cody looked thoughtful for a moment. "Depends on who you pissed off."

She shivered. Yeah, that was certainly true. She'd pushed hard for justice for Mark, and she hadn't made friends over that. Not that anyone wanted an agent's death to go unpunished, but sometimes there was more at stake than immediate arrests.

She knew that, and she was fine with it. But it was time to bring down Conti's organization. Past time. He was a cancer that needed cutting out before it was too late.

"You hungry?" Cody asked, snapping her out of her thoughts.

She blinked at him. Her stomach answered on cue with a growl. "I could eat."

"There should be energy bars in the console—but if you want something more substantial, I know of a diner not too far from here. I can get us some takeout."

She processed everything he said, looking for the angle—and then she cursed silently. There was no angle. He was helping her. Taking care of her. Because he was HOT, and a SEAL. She wasn't used to it, didn't know how to act.

"Sure. Sounds good."

Fifteen minutes later, he pulled up in front of a diner and switched off the ignition. She watched with interest—and a touch of disappointment—as he pocketed the keys. But really, what would she accomplish by ditching him here? She'd be alone, and there was no one she could call. She didn't think Badger was out to hurt her, but if she called him for help, he'd have to get other agents involved—and that's where the uncertainty lay.

"What do you want? Burger? Chicken sandwich?"

"Club sandwich if they've got it."

"Fries?"

"Definitely."

"Something to drink?"

"Sweet tea, but since I know they don't have it because nobody understands how to make it outside of the South, I'll take water."

He snorted a laugh. "Was that actually humor? Are you softening toward me?"

Warmth suffused her for some silly reason. "You're turning me into a puddle, Cody McCormick. I'm as soft as a stick of butter in a cast-iron skillet."

This time his laugh was more pronounced. "Careful, Miranda. You might actually like me before this is over if you aren't."

She crossed her arms in mock defense. "No way."

He opened the door and stepped out. "Way," he said, grinning.

Her pulse jumped as he shut the door and strolled into the diner. Handsome asshole.

CHAPTER SEVEN

THEY REACHED THE designated safe house around one in the morning. It wasn't much more than a shack really, located in the middle of an arid landscape. They weren't far from the Grand Canyon, though far enough. The house was small, tucked away on a plot of land where nothing grew other than scrub and cactus.

Cody stood in the kitchen and dialed his HOT brothers. Viking answered this time.

"Good to hear," he said when Cody informed him they'd arrived at the safe house. There was a pause. "We did a little digging on Miranda Lockwood."

Cody watched the bedroom door where Miranda had disappeared. She'd been quiet when they'd arrived. Lost in her own thoughts. He'd actually thought she was warming up after the visit to the diner, but she'd gone silent again as the hours ticked by.

"Yeah? And?"

"And the CIA nearly had a shit fit when her name

was mentioned."

Cody's neck prickled. "Really? Did they say why?"

Viking sighed. "You aren't going to like it. They say she's gone rogue. Say she's dangerous and not to be trusted. They also want to know where she is so they can bring her in."

The prickling sensation grew stronger. "Did you tell them?"

"No. But man, Mendez wasn't happy when that phone call was done. He looked like he'd swallowed a nest of angry hornets."

Cody didn't like to think of Colonel Mendez unhappy. He'd seen the skipper angry once, and it had been memorable. Not something you wanted to call down on yourself, that's for sure. The dude was legendary in HOT—and legendary in spec ops.

Since Cody's team had joined HOT—the first SEAL team to do so—he'd learned a lot about the Army colonel in charge, though not as much as there was to know. He suspected that nobody would ever know the full story of Mendez. The legend was enough.

"Mendez doesn't believe she's turned rogue, does he?" It was intuition that told him that much, but he knew it was true. If Mendez had believed it, Cody and Miranda wouldn't have made it this far. They'd have been picked up hours ago.

"Nope. But there's something going on, something big, and you're going to have to lie low out there for a few days while we figure it out."

"Roger that—but is this something we're officially involved in now?"

"Officially? No. But we aren't turning her over. Yet."

Yet. That was the word Cody didn't care for. "I don't think she's gone rogue. I think she's scared of something."

"We'll do what we can. You know that."

"Yeah."

"Hey, Cage says if you didn't want to go to the wedding, you could have just said so."

Cody laughed. "Tell him I'll be there." It was a week away. Surely he wouldn't still be holed up in the desert with a sexy CIA agent by then. HOT would figure out what was going on, and it would all be over.

"Hooyah. We'll be in touch."

Cody hung up and went over to the bedroom door. He stood there for a long moment before knocking. When there was no answer, he knocked again, his pulse kicking up. Surely she wouldn't run out on him now. It would be foolish to try to escape out here in the middle of nowhere. He had the keys, so she couldn't take the truck. And leaving on foot was a suicide mission.

Still, he shoved the door open when there was no answer. It took a moment, but the trickle of water in the shower told him where she'd gone. He had to be sure, however. He didn't really know Miranda Lockwood, didn't know that she wouldn't try to escape. She could have turned the shower on to throw him off his game.

Cody strode toward the bathroom door. It was open a few inches, and there was steam rolling through it. He heard nothing beyond the water, however. Nothing to indicate there was anyone in the shower.

He stood, straining to hear her—and then he pushed the door open all the way. At the same moment, the shower stopped and the curtain squealed open on plastic rings. Miranda blinked, her golden eyes wide, her body glistening with moisture.

He couldn't tear his eyes away. Her blond hair was piled on top of her head, the ends damp and clinging to her face. Her breasts were firm and round, her nipples stiff in the cool air wafting over them after the hot shower. Her waist dipped inward before her hips flared out in an exaggerated curve. Her skin was creamy, pale. She trimmed. That was his first thought when his gaze landed on the triangle between her legs. Her hair was short, golden, trimmed almost bare but not quite. He could see her pussy lips, the pink clitoris between them.

His dick grew instantly hard.

"What the fuck?" she demanded, grasping a towel and hiding her assets.

It was too late for his dick, but he swallowed and tried to regain his equilibrium. "I thought you'd tried to escape."

Her face was red, and not just from the shower he'd bet. She wrapped the towel tightly around her and held on to it as if he planned to rip it away in the next moment.

"Why the hell would I do that? Where would I go? In case you haven't noticed, there's nothing but desert in all directions."

He had noticed. But it was dark, so he wasn't sure she had. "I don't know what you're thinking, sunshine. Could be anything."

"If I was planning to run away, I wouldn't slink off into the night. I'd put my fucking gun to your head and demand the keys, asshole."

He held up both hands, partly to keep her gaze from straying to his crotch. If she saw his response to her naked body, she'd be even more pissed. "Hear you loud and clear, babe."

"Fine. Now get out and let me dry off. And don't call me babe."

He backed away, then stopped and met her angry gaze again. "Just for the record, you put a gun to my head and this isn't going to end well for you."

Because it had to be said. She was a trained operative, but so was he. And he wasn't going down easy.

She stared at him evenly. "I don't plan on it, cowboy. For now, you're all I've got."

CHAPTER EIGHT

MIRANDA DIDN'T MOVE for a long minute after he disappeared through the door. Her heart pounded and her skin prickled with heat—but that was probably just the shower. Except it was cold now that the water was off and the air was wafting over her body.

Whatever. She was not ashamed if a man saw her naked. Hell, she'd gone topless for the job before. Worn a teeny tiny G-string and danced on a bar—not only when she was eighteen and stripping for cash, but also as an undercover agent. She had no problem showing her body. Never had.

So why the heat of embarrassment now? Lord have mercy, she wanted to clap her hands to her cheeks and see if they were as hot as they felt.

And she knew why she was hot, didn't she? The way he'd looked at her—and the way she'd responded when he did. The heat. The sizzle in the air. Whoa and damn. If nipples were capable of standing up and saying *Howdy, stranger,* then hers sure had. Not only that, but she'd felt the slickness of arousal between her legs.

He'd been aroused too. She hadn't missed that. How could she? My God, he was huge. The outline of his hard cock against his jeans had been impressive. She'd wanted to see more, but thank God she had more sense than that. She was capable of casual sex for sex's sake—wouldn't be the first time—but this wasn't the right time for it. She needed to keep her wits, not lose her mind over a Hollywood-handsome SEAL with a big dick.

She almost laughed. Earlier, she'd thought he probably had a little dick just because that's the way the world worked. But of course he didn't. Every inch of him was perfectly appealing.

And she had no business thinking about it.

Miranda toweled off, unclipped her hair from on top of her head—thank God she'd found a hair clip in the drawer—and slipped into the jeans and T-shirt that had been waiting for her in the Dodge. Too bad they hadn't thought about providing her with pajamas.

She'd searched the drawers and closet in the bedroom and they were empty. Well, except for sheets and blankets. She could have wrapped one of those around her instead of getting dressed again, she supposed.

She stared at herself in the mirror, at her red cheeks and bright eyes. Lord, what was Cody going to think if she walked out there like this?

She turned on the cold water and doused her cheeks. It helped somewhat. She took a deep breath and went out into the small living room. The house was tiny with a galley kitchen, dining nook, and microscopic living room. She hadn't explored beyond the first bedroom and bath she came to, but she hoped like hell there was another. Because if she had to share with Mister Tall, Dark, and Sinfully Sexy— Well, it didn't bear thinking about.

Cody looked up from where he sat on the couch, his gaze gliding coolly over her form. She couldn't help but glance at his jeans for evidence of that hard-on—but it was gone. She didn't know whether to feel relief or disappointment about that.

"Everything okay?" he asked. As if he hadn't just seen her naked. As if he hadn't had wood.

"Fine. You?" She sank onto the chair opposite and pulled her knees up. She should probably go to bed, but she was too keyed up.

"The CIA says you're a rogue agent."

And that took all the fight right out of her. Her chest felt as if someone had wrapped a hand around her heart and squeezed. "What?" She barely got the word out.

"That's what they told my commander."

Her throat ached and her eyes stung. "It's not true."

"Why would they say that, Miranda?"

She had no idea. "I don't know. I told you the mission was top secret—I was supposed to infiltrate Victor Conti's operation. I was going in through the porn side."

His eyes flashed and his jaw tightened. "The porn side? Just what were you planning to do?"

She swallowed. "I wasn't going to be an actress if that's what you're thinking. I was, uh, someone who could get girls for the films. Fresh, new faces."

He looked fierce in that moment. "A talent scout? How the fuck do you know he wouldn't have wanted a performance from you just to prove you knew what you were doing?"

Her pulse quickened. "I didn't know that at all. Maybe he would have."

"You were prepared to fuck him? Or fuck an actor on camera?"

She pressed her hands to her temples. "I was prepared to make him *think* I'd fuck him—or an actor, yes. It wasn't going that far though. I wasn't going to let it."

"Jesus." Cody swore long and hard. "Is that what the CIA does these days? Pimp their fucking agents to porn purveyors?"

"I volunteered." She licked her bottom lip. "It was the only way in. We've tried other ways—they didn't work."

An understatement considering Mark was dead.

"You must want to see him taken down pretty badly."

Miranda closed her eyes and bit down on the inside of her cheek. How much could she say to this man? On the other hand, what could she lose? Her own people said she was a rogue agent. She took the burner phone from her pocket and flipped it open. Then she dialed Badger's number.

"Mandy, thank God."

"Is it true?" she demanded. Her gaze met Cody's. He was watching her sympathetically, and that made her breath quicken a fraction.

"Is what true?"

"I'm a rogue agent now? I need to be taken down and handed over before I do any damage?"

"Shit." She heard him blow out a breath and she knew he was smoking. "I'm trying to fix this, Mandy, I swear."

"What's there to fix? Someone betrayed me to Conti. Someone wants me brought in. What do you think the chances are I'll come out of it alive if I'm taken now?"

"It's not like that. I swear it's not. Come in and we'll work on it together. Show good faith and it'll all turn out right."

Her eyes stung. Good faith? "'Bye, Badger. Give my love to Susan."

She ended the call with his voice fairly screaming through the line. But there was nothing he could say. No way he could convince her. She dropped the phone and put her fingers against the sides of her head, pressing as if she could stop the pain from growing any worse.

"You okay?"

She couldn't look at him. "No."

He blew out a breath. And then he was moving. When he sat beside her and dragged her against him, she stiffened for a second. But he didn't do anything inappropriate. He held her loosely, allowing her room to escape if she desired.

She did not want to escape. Instead, she turned her face into his broad chest and breathed him in. He smelled good. Clean and masculine. It had been so long since she'd let a man hold her. So damn long.

"Why don't you believe what they're saying about me?" she asked, her voice muffled against the fabric of his T-shirt. Really, this was completely wrong and so not her—but it felt too good, and she was at such a low point that she wanted someone else to be strong for a moment.

His fingers stroked over her hair. The touch was light, but it went deep into her soul for some crazy reason.

"Maybe I'm wrong, but *rogue* says to me that someone no longer plays by the rules. That they have an agenda beyond the official agenda and they are willing to do anything to get it. Would someone who'd turned against the

CIA care whether or not her hostage lived? Or would she kill him as soon as he'd served his purpose?"

She sucked in a breath. "She'd let him live if there was no point in killing him. And there wasn't. You got me out of the Venetian. That's all I needed."

"Yeah, well, you could have forced me into the parking garage and into a vehicle and then dumped me along the way."

"You took my gun. I couldn't do any of it." She sniffed.

He chuckled softly. "True. But let me have my fantasy, okay? So you didn't shoot me then—and you didn't take any of the opportunities you've had since I returned your clip to leave me for dead."

She twisted her fingers into the fabric of his T-shirt. It was much too intimate, but she liked it. "I'm biding my time," she said. "You're still useful."

He laughed out loud this time, and a wave of relief washed over her that he'd found it funny. Yeah, she was a smart-ass and sometimes it went too far. Maybe she shouldn't have said it at all—but he'd been amused, and that was a good thing.

"I live to serve, baby."

She pushed back enough that she could see his face. He was so close, so damned appealing, and warmth flooded her. Eyes the color of the desert sky stared back at her.

Her gaze dropped to his mouth. Those lips begged to be kissed. They were firm, smooth, and sensual. She imagined them against hers, imagined how they would feel and taste.

"Miranda."

She snapped her attention to his eyes again. They

were still blue, still clear—but now they gleamed hotly, their depths intense.

"Yes?" She tried to make the word innocent, clueless.

"I just saw you naked. I'm not likely to forget that sight anytime soon. And while I didn't come over here to be a douche and make a move on you while you're upset, if you keep looking at me like I'm something you'd like to saddle up and ride, I'm going to oblige your curiosity."

Her heart was in her throat, fluttering away like a moth's wings beating against the jar someone had trapped it in. She didn't know this man at all, and yet a part of her very much wanted to go there with him.

Crazy.

"I'm sorry," she said, pushing away from him even more.

He took his arm from around her and put his hands together in his lap. "Don't apologize. I like the way you look at me. But I'm only human, Miranda. And I'm pretty sure this isn't what you really want right now."

"I don't know what I want," she admitted.

He pushed to his feet and went over to the tiny kitchen where he pulled a beer out of the fridge. "How about one of these?"

"Sure."

He got another one out, popped the tops, and brought them back. After handing her one, he took the seat opposite her again. And yes, she glanced at his dick to see if it was hard. It was, which only made her wetter.

"I don't think you've gone rogue," he said, propping a foot on the coffee table. Hiding the evidence of his arousal, sad to say. "But you're in over your head, that's for sure."

"Do you think this is something HOT can sort out?" Because she was done believing in the agency. Done believing that even Badger could do anything for her this time. She was on her own for the first time in years, and she didn't quite know how she was going to get out of this mess without help.

He took a sip of the beer. "I think it's possible, yeah."

She played with her bottle but didn't drink it. "I hope you're right. Because I think if you don't, I'm a dead woman."

His eyes flashed. "Not on my watch, babe. Promise."

CHAPTER NINE

SHE WAS QUIET again. Lost in her own thoughts. Cody watched her surreptitiously. He didn't miss the way she toyed with her beer or the way she frowned as she gazed at seemingly nothing. She was troubled.

And why wouldn't she be? Someone had betrayed her. Her own agency had turned against her. She was a rogue on the run now, a wild card until and unless HOT could figure out what was going on and who had set her up.

Cody blinked. He'd never really considered that she *was* a rogue, but why not? He didn't know her, didn't know what she was capable of. Anyone could snap when given the right incentive. Just look at his mother.

"Do you trust this Badger person?" he asked, and her head came up.

"Yes, of course."

But was that a hint of uncertainty in her voice? Or just irritation?

"Tell me about the operation, Miranda."

She nibbled the inside of her lip, and his groin tightened at that tiny maneuver.

"I already told you."

"No, not really. You told me what it was for. You didn't tell me the plan."

She blew out a breath. And then she shook her head. "I honestly don't think I'm supposed to tell you any more than I already have."

"I'm pretty much the only one who believes you right now. You sure you want to keep me in the dark?"

She laid her head back against the couch cushion and fixed him with a look. "You're wrong, you know that?"

"Enlighten me."

"I *am* a rogue, at least by your definition. You said it was someone who had an agenda beyond the official agenda—and yes, I do. This is personal to me, Cody. I volunteered because I have a personal stake. Hell, I pushed for the op in the first place."

It wasn't the first time she'd said his name, but this time the sound of it on her lips made his balls start to ache.

"I've been an agent for four years now. I was lucky to get in, quite honestly. I had a mentor—" She swallowed and dropped her gaze for a moment. "A man who saved me from myself when I was eighteen. He found someone to look after me, someone to make sure I got my GED and became a productive citizen. He was my idol in many ways, and I wanted to make him proud."

She didn't have to say that man was an agent. It was clear.

"We were lovers," she said.

Cody didn't like the stab of feeling in his gut at that

news.

"But we weren't in love or anything. Or Mark wasn't. I was certain I loved him for a time, but he didn't return it. He cared for me though. We stopped being lovers a long time ago, but the friendship never went away. He got assigned to infiltrate Conti's organization. He worked it for months, and he was good at it. I was his contact on the outside. He was so close to breaking their code, to knowing the whole operation—and then his car blew up one morning when he was supposed to be meeting me to pass information."

"I'm sorry, Miranda."

"Thank you. I know it's the nature of what we do, the possibility in every assignment—but it was still a shock." She sniffed, but she wasn't crying. "Of course he was killed by someone in Conti's organization—but it wasn't Conti. In all the intel afterward, he seemed stunned by it. He never knew Mark was an agent. But someone did, and they not only eliminated him, they also never told their boss."

"So you weren't just trying to complete what Mark started, you were also trying to find out who killed him."

She clasped her hands in her lap. "Yes. It was a long shot, but I had to try."

"Did anyone else know what you were really after?"

"Badger. They were best friends. Went to college together. He wants Mark's killer as much as I do."

"He also wants you to come in."

"He means well. He thinks he can protect me."

"But you don't believe he can." It wasn't a question.

She sighed. "In many ways, I don't know what to believe anymore. But I'm pretty sure that going in would not work out in my favor just yet." Her golden eyes were sad, troubled. "I'm putting my faith in your group, Cody. You're all I have right now."

He didn't know why he did it, but he reached out and took her hand in his. Squeezed. She didn't try to remove it. "I'm not quitting, sunshine. None of us are quitting. We'll clear your name."

It was a tall order, but goddammit, he wasn't giving up until they had. Miranda Lockwood might be a lot of things, but a traitor to her country was not one of them.

"Of all the shitty luck I've had today, I'm beginning to believe that choosing you in the Venetian was not part of it."

Cody grinned. "Of course it wasn't. You're going to remember this day as the day you met me for the rest of your life. Probably name your first kid after me or something."

She frowned, but he could see the hint of a smile in it. "You're insane."

"Quite possibly."

She yawned, her jaw cracking. "I need to go to bed."

He stood and stretched. "Yeah, me too. But sunshine?"

Her eyes looked sleepy. "Yes?"

"There's only one bedroom."

CHAPTER TEN

"THIS STRIKES ME as a bad idea," Miranda said, standing in the entry to the bedroom. She was wearing one of Cody's T-shirts for a nightie because she had nothing else, and it suddenly felt far too short even though it came to midthigh.

He was wearing a pair of athletic shorts, but his chest was bare. And that was definitely a problem, because whoa and damn, that was a mighty fine chest. He had a tattoo on his left pectoral muscle. She realized a moment later that it was the Navy SEAL trident. He also had a tattoo on his shoulder—she noticed it when he turned around to finish pulling the covers down—that said *Where None Dare*. The HOT motto, though not many would know that.

Miranda swallowed as he turned back to her. His blue eyes appeared placid, but then she saw they really were not. Still waters run deep and all that. His gaze slipped over her, lingering on her bare legs for a moment. His eyes were… hot. And the look in them made her tremble.

She tried to remember how Mark had looked at her. If she'd ever trembled because of it. He'd been tall, brown-haired with a hint of silver at the temples, and his eyes were green. They'd been interesting eyes. Eyes that had seen much and yet gave nothing away.

But he'd never, not once, looked at her with the heat that Cody did.

Why not?

"It's the only option," he said, interrupting her thoughts. "If you want to get any sleep, that is. You can try the couch—but it's pretty damned uncomfortable."

That it was. It was old and lumpy and the arms were hard. She wasn't very tall, but she couldn't stretch across the whole couch. And it was pretty damn clear that *he* wasn't going to sleep on the couch. No way would he fit.

She went over to the queen-sized bed and fluffed up the pillow on her side before primly getting under the covers. "Stay on your side, cowboy, and we'll get along just fine."

He chuckled as he tossed his pillow against the headboard. "Sunshine, it won't be a problem. I sleep in worse conditions and closer quarters with people who aren't nearly as pretty as you—and not one of them has ever complained that I'm incapable of respecting personal space."

She sniffed. "Unless there's something you aren't telling me, I don't think those SEALs are your type—whereas I might be."

He laughed outright this time, and she felt herself coloring. Really, could she sound any more like a frightened virgin maiden with a serious stick up her ass?

"Yeah, you're definitely my type. You've got all the

parts I like best—and I've seen those parts, so I know how magnificent they are. But unless you ask me to come out and play, I know how to keep my dick in my pants and my hands to myself. You've got nothing to worry about."

He sank onto the bed, but instead of getting under the covers, he stayed on top. Miranda flicked off her light and closed her eyes. She was tired—more tired than she'd realized—and yet sleep was still elusive. Ten minutes went by. Then fifteen.

Her mind was too busy concentrating on the sounds the man beside her made—not that he made much sound at all, but every shift of his body on the mattress, no matter how slight, created a disturbance that rolled through her. He was also reading on his phone. She could tell because of the light pressing against her eyes.

"Why were you in Vegas?" she finally asked, needing to hear the sound of his voice. Needing to know she wasn't on her own. She wasn't afraid of being alone, not usually, but now that she'd been betrayed by someone in the agency, she felt completely without connections to anything or anyone. She didn't like that feeling.

It's your own fault, a voice whispered in her head. *You broke ties with your sisters, your parents.*

Yes, she had. And she didn't regret it. Not usually.

"I was visiting family."

She opened her eyes and gazed up at his handsome profile. "In the Venetian?"

He was silent for a moment. "I was looking for someone."

It hit her then that perhaps he had a girlfriend, or even a wife. What if he'd been looking for a woman? And she'd interrupted him. Taken him away before he could meet whomever he was meeting.

"I'm sorry if I ruined your plans," she said. It was a lame apology—and a late one—but it was the best she could do. Though if she'd taken him away from another woman, she wasn't sorry for it. She should be, but she wasn't.

"No plans." He sighed. "I was looking for my mother. She has a habit of disappearing into the Vegas scene and upsetting my grandparents."

She didn't know what to say to that. "I'm sorry I interrupted your search then."

And she really was. It was clear he wasn't happy about what his mother had done. If she hadn't interfered, he might even now be reunited with his mom.

"Don't be. She doesn't want to be found anyway. Plus I'm fucking tired of looking every time she goes off the rails. If it weren't for Gramps and Grandma, I wouldn't do it."

"My mother is an alcoholic," she said and then wanted to bite her tongue. Where the fuck had that come from? She didn't share those things with anyone. Not ever. It was a life she'd left behind, a life she didn't want or need.

"Mine probably is too, but she's always hidden it so well. She can stop for weeks at a time. Then she inevitably goes on another bender, and the shit hits the fan."

"I don't remember my mother ever *not* drinking," Miranda said, her throat tight. The utter dysfunction of the Lockwood family as her mother drank all day and her father came home with coal staining his skin, spitting mad and ready to tear into his wife and kids, was seared into her soul forever. The utter fucking misery of it all would never be washed away. That was why she'd never gone back again. Why she couldn't.

"She hit the bottle all day long," she continued. "Whatever cheap shit she could beg, borrow, or steal. And when she couldn't get her vodka, she'd drink cough syrup for the alcohol content. It wasn't a good substitute though."

"I'm sorry you had to grow up that way. It's not fair to the kids."

"No." She swallowed the hard lump in her throat. It was dark, except for his phone, which made the situation seem cozy and safe. She knew it wasn't, and yet she wanted to talk. For once in her life, she wanted to share it with someone. Blame it on the stress of her current circumstances.

"I have five sisters. We were left alone a lot, and that's fine when you're kids in the country. There's plenty to do when your life revolves around fields and streams. We'd take off in the morning and wouldn't come home until late. Daddy worked the coal mines, and his hours were erratic. I think I sometimes went for days without seeing an adult, truth be known."

"Mark saved you from that life?"

Had he? Or had he merely encouraged her in the right direction when she needed it most? "I left home at eighteen. I didn't have a plan, not really. Other kids were going to college, but how the hell was I going to afford that?" She shook her head. "The only way out for me was to leave. I should have joined the military, I see that now, but instead I decided to strip and earn my fortune that way." She couldn't help but snort a laugh at the naive teenager she'd been.

"I was there for a week before things went to hell.

One of the clients wanted a bit more than a lap dance. When I said no, he tried to force me into another room. I have no doubt he'd have raped me. But Mark was there, and he stopped the guy. Then he bundled me away and I never went back. Not even to collect my last paycheck."

Cody swore. "Good thing he was there."

"Yes." She sighed and closed her eyes. Her skin prickled with heat. She thought about tossing the covers off and then decided it wasn't a good idea really. Not with Cody here, and not with the electric hum simmering deep inside her veins. She felt like one hot look might set her off.

"Do you get back home much?" he asked, and everything inside her went still.

"There's nothing to go back for. My mother is still an alcoholic, and my father is still an asshole. I talk to my oldest sister—nothing has changed and nothing ever will."

Miranda frowned. Why the effing hell was she still talking about this? It only made her seem weak and pitiful—and she would *never* be either of those things.

"I get it. I go back for my grandparents. My mom—well, she's a good person deep down, but she's selfish and miserable, and she makes everyone around her miserable. It's more than I want to deal with when I'm taking a break from the realities of the job."

"Exactly."

She loved that he understood. Mark had often asked why she didn't go home for a visit, why she didn't try. He'd believed she needed that connection, but then he'd been an orphan who'd never known his own parents. He and his sister had been raised by an aunt and uncle who apparently weren't the warmest people on the planet.

He'd thought her parents were simply flawed people, not toxic destroyers of everything good in life, because that's what he needed to believe about parents in general.

"I'm still sorry I interrupted your evening, Cody. And sorry if I took you away from visiting with your grandparents."

"Honestly, sunshine? I love them and love seeing them, but getting kidnapped by you and being on the run from Victor Conti—and the CI-fucking-A—is a lot more fun."

She wanted to laugh but she managed not to. "You have a warped idea of fun."

"Oh, I have plenty of other ideas about what's fun," he said, his voice a lovely deep purr that strummed against her nerve endings. "Let me know if you want to hear them."

CHAPTER ELEVEN

SHE DID WANT to hear them. Badly. Her body sizzled with heat, her pussy growing wet and achy with need. It had been so long. Too long. She wanted a man, wanted the comfort that kind of closeness could give. She also wanted an orgasm that someone else made happen. She was tired of getting herself off in the loneliness of an empty bed.

When was the last time she'd slept with a man? It was over a year ago, that much was certain. She and Mark hadn't been together anymore, not like that. She'd started dating a guy, another agent—the sex had been decent but not memorable. They'd gone their separate ways, and that was the end of that. It was difficult, quite honestly, to find time—or the right sort of person—in the job she was in.

Too hilarious that she'd been playing a pornography talent agent in order to insert herself into Conti's operations. If she'd had to be on set for any of that stuff, she'd have probably gone straight to the adult toy store and bought a vibrator after it was over.

Her breathing grew heavier, her nipples tingling as they beaded tight under the T-shirt. All she had to do was reach out and touch him. Just touch him, give the signal, and he'd end this drought for her. Hell, even if he sucked, at least he had a big cock—which would probably be enough to send her over the edge once he slid it inside her.

He'd gone back to reading on his phone, clearly not believing she would take him up on that offer.

And really, she couldn't. It was a nice thought—a thought that made her whimper—but this was not the time to start messing around with a Navy SEAL. She needed her wits about her—and she needed him to have his. Sex was a distraction.

The light on his phone winked out, and then he laid it on the bedside table. He settled down beside her but not touching her.

"Try to sleep," he said into the stillness. "We're safe here for now, I promise."

"What if somebody remembers seeing us switch to the Dodge? What if Conti's men are right behind us?"

"It's possible, sure. But they won't have seen where we went, Miranda. The Dodge is equipped with a signal scrambler. Nobody's going to be able to pinpoint our location using the GPS."

"I hope you're right."

"I am. Sleep tonight. Tomorrow we'll find out what we need to do next."

She lay in the dark and listened. When his breathing evened out, she experienced a moment of elation. She could leave if she wanted. Take the truck and go. But where would she run? Who would help her? She couldn't turn to Badger. He would want to help, of course, but if she was compromised, then so was he—which meant she couldn't trust that any communication she had with him wouldn't be intercepted.

She turned onto her side and let her gaze slide over the form of the man beside her. No, she wasn't leaving him. For good or bad, he was her only hope right now. It was such an odd thought. She didn't know him. They'd never worked together. But from the moment she'd pushed her pistol into his side, he'd been calm and deliberate in his actions.

Yeah, he looked like a hot cowboy in his boots and faded jeans—except that he needed a hat, though she was kind of glad he didn't have one. He'd be much too appealing with a cowboy hat.

As if he wasn't already too appealing. Miranda worked on her breathing, tried to calm the thudding of her heart. It was as if she'd drank an entire pot of coffee when she hadn't had any at all. Jesus.

She turned onto her back and folded her hands over her middle, closing her eyes and praying for sleep. But she knew it wasn't going to come. She was too keyed up, her brain spinning as she tried to process everything that had happened in the past few hours.

Who would want to discredit her? And why? Why would this person betray her to Conti?

Because he or she has been paid off, that's why. It's not personal.

No, it probably wasn't personal. She was just the one caught in the middle when the shit hit the fan.

She had been lying there for a long time, listening to Cody breathe, trying to sleep and figure out what her next move should be, when Cody's body began to jerk. He twitched and moaned, calling out once or twice, though it was nothing intelligible.

She recognized bad dreams. She had them herself sometimes. You didn't do a job like this and not get nightmares. It was only if the nightmares interfered with your life that they became a problem.

She thought about waking him, but that might not be a good idea. Instead, she decided to ease out of the bed and give him space. If it went on too long, she'd wake him. She flipped back the covers and slipped a leg out from under them.

And then a hand clamped down on her arm, scaring her enough to make her squeak. But it didn't stop there. He dragged her toward him and then flipped her so she was on her back and he was on top of her, his entire length pressing into her. His hard, hot, incredibly fit body. Pressing. Into. Her.

Miranda bit back a moan even though common sense told her that wasn't the proper reaction at the moment.

"Cody," she said, keeping her voice as calm and soothing as possible. Not daring to move in case he decided she needed more restraining than she was already getting. "It's Miranda. Your CIA pal. The one you're helping escape from the bad guys. You're dreaming, cowboy."

He didn't say anything for a long moment. And then he seemed to shake himself. "Miranda?"

"Yep, it's me. How's it going, buddy?"

He shuddered. It wasn't the best maneuver for her sanity because he was at least half hard from the contact and his cock was pressing into her mound. Right up against all those sensitive nerve endings. Not to mention that the T-shirt she was wearing had gotten twisted and dragged upward so that everything from her belly button down was exposed.

And her cotton underwear wasn't much of a barrier between them.

"I was dreaming. Sorry."

"Yeah, I figured. Everything okay?"

He moved his head in the darkness. Shaking it? "It will be."

She lifted her arms and put her hands on his biceps. Touching him gently. Lightly. But her fingers trembled as she did so. Was she that out of practice? Or was it him and this effect he had on her?

"Do you want to talk about it?"

He stilled at her words. Or maybe it was her touch. She wasn't sure.

"No," he grated.

She thought he might make a move to get off her, let her go. But he didn't. He stayed where he was, his body pressing hers into the mattress, and a shiver of anticipation rolled over her. She wet her lips, her pulse racing, her body humming.

"What do you want, Cody?"

"Honestly? I want to strip you naked and make you scream my name."

Her belly twisted with hunger. Her pussy throbbed as another surge of heat rolled through her. She ran her hand up his arm, into his hair. He was warm, so warm. Solid and comforting.

"Maybe I want that too."

She felt his response instantly. His cock pressed against her, harder than before, and she tried to wiggle her legs apart so she could shift her hips and apply the pressure just where she wanted it. But he didn't let her move.

"You don't know what you're saying, Miranda. Your life has been turned upside down, and you're reacting in ways you probably wouldn't otherwise."

She put her hand over his mouth to stop any other ridiculous words from exiting. "I'm pretty sure I'm a grown-ass woman, Cody McCormick. I can make up my own mind about who I fuck. It's just sex, for God's sake. We aren't talking about a marriage proposal here, or a future together. I'm not so weak-minded that I fall apart at the first sign of trouble and screw whatever red-blooded male is available, you know."

She took her hand off his mouth and was rewarded with laughter. Not quite the reaction she'd expected.

"You do realize what you just said is pretty much every man's wet dream? No-strings sex with a gorgeous woman." He shook his head. "Is it fucking Christmas or what?"

"Listen here, smart-ass. I can't sleep, I haven't had sex in over a year, I'm horny as hell, and you're not only male, but you're pretty hot too. So either shut up and kiss me, or get the fuck out of here and leave me alone. Because I am done sleeping in the same bed with you unless you keep your promise to make me scream."

CHAPTER TWELVE

CODY SHUDDERED. HE shouldn't do this, God knows he shouldn't, but he wasn't going to say no. He should have gotten off her when he'd woken and realized he was pinning her down, but he hadn't been able to make himself move. She'd felt too good beneath him. The effects of the dream were still dragging him down into a pit of despair, and Miranda was the only bright spot he could see. Losing himself in sex with her would chase the darkness away, at least for a little while.

With a groan, he lowered his head and captured her mouth. She opened to him eagerly, her tongue sliding against his with sensual abandon. The bolt of lust rocketing through him wasn't surprising. The wave of tenderness for the woman beneath him was.

Whether he took a woman to bed after knowing her for a few hours or a few weeks, emotion was never involved. It was a transaction to him. A mutually satisfying exploration of bodies. Sometimes he saw the same woman again. Sometimes once was enough.

He had no idea which it was going to be with Miranda, but the tenderness was new and unexpected. Quite possibly because he felt sorry for her and everything she'd gone through. She was in trouble and he wanted to help her, and maybe that added something to the mix that he hadn't accounted for.

Whatever the reason, he wasn't stopping to explore his feelings. Fuck that. Besides, it wasn't going to last. Once he relieved this searing tension in his balls, his head would clear and he could think again.

He lifted himself up enough to get his hands on the T-shirt she'd worn to bed, and then he dragged it up and over her head. Her arms went around his neck again and she pulled him down, her eager mouth seeking his. He kissed her hard, deep, his fingers sliding up to cup a breast. She moaned and arched into him as he flicked her nipple.

Damn, she was sensitive. He broke the kiss and took her nipple into his mouth, flicking his tongue against the tight, fat peak. Miranda writhed beneath him, her fingers curling into his shoulders almost painfully.

Jesus. She'd said it had been more than a year. He couldn't imagine a woman as beautiful as her going without physical contact, but who knew why people did what they did sometimes? He thought of her with Conti earlier, of the look on her face as she'd approached him. She'd been tough and determined and scared all at once.

Thank God he'd let her steer him outside. That he hadn't disarmed her then and there and turned her over to the men who wanted her.

"Oh," she gasped as he grazed his teeth over her nipple. "Yes, like that. Please, like that."

He cupped both her breasts and pushed them together, giving her nipples the attention they needed with his tongue and teeth.

"Oh my God," she moaned, arching into him, her hips lifting as she rode the bulge in his athletic shorts. He shifted away from her and she whimpered.

But he didn't want her reaching orgasm that way. He wanted to give it to her, not have her find it while rubbing her clit against his hardness.

"You have perfect nipples," he told her before sucking hard on one while she mewled. He let it pop from his mouth and then did the same to the other one.

He couldn't see her as well as he would like in the darkness, but he didn't want to take the time to turn on the light. Maybe it would break the spell if he did. Maybe she wouldn't want to keep going, or maybe he wouldn't—though he doubted that very much.

But he wanted to see her body again. The glimpse he'd gotten of her earlier had been amazing, but he wanted more. He wanted to watch her eyes dilate with pleasure, watch as she bit her lip and moaned. He wanted to see her reaction when he slid deep inside her.

It wasn't going to happen though. Maybe next time. Assuming there was a next time. He was smart enough to realize that once might be it. No matter what she said, she might regret that she'd crossed this line with him tonight.

A wave of fierceness rolled through him. He didn't want her to regret it, goddammit. And he was going to do everything he could to make sure she didn't.

Swiftly, he hooked his fingers into her panties and yanked them off. She lifted her legs, helping him out. Their eyes met, tangled for a moment. And then he settled between her legs and pushed her knees apart.

He tested her with his fingers first, sliding them down along the seam of her sex. She was wetter than he'd imagined, the folds of her pussy swollen with desire, and a shot of primal need lanced through him.

"Do you want me to lick you, sunshine?"

Her breath caught. "God, yes. I'd make a deal with the devil himself if that's what it took."

Cody couldn't help but chuckle. She amused him even when he didn't expect it.

"No deal with the devil. But Miranda, if you change your mind about the rest of this after you come, I'm going to cross you off my Christmas card list forever."

It was her turn to laugh. "You don't have a Christmas card list, cowboy. You're a manly man, and your kind doesn't send cards."

"Damn, you got me there—but honey," he said, his tone serious, "if you don't want to do this, tell me. I'll stop."

She reached down and threaded a hand into his hair. Something about her touch sent a shiver down his spine. A good shiver.

"You need to stop talking and start licking, big boy. And then, once I've recovered from what is sure to be an awesome orgasm, I'll return the favor. Promise."

CHAPTER THIRTEEN

HER HEART WAS in her throat. Her pussy ached. Her stomach churned. She needed him to touch her, and she was afraid he wouldn't. Afraid he'd have an attack of nobility or something that would make him insist she didn't really want this and he wasn't going to take advantage.

Really, men could be so silly sometimes. She held her breath, waiting. And then his fingers glided against her again, and she hissed as his thumb skated over her clitoris. The aftershocks sizzled through her like a flash fire.

"You're so wet for me, Miranda. I love it."

Before she could reply, he spread her with his thumbs and touched his tongue to her clit. She saw stars. Her hands automatically went to his head, her fingers shoving into his hair.

He hummed a laugh, and the stars intensified. It wasn't going to take long at this rate, which both excited and disappointed her at the same time. Hell yes, she wanted to come.

But not so fast. She wanted this incredible feeling of excitement and tension to last longer than five seconds.

It wasn't in the cards. He sucked her clit into his mouth the way he had her nipples—and she exploded. He tugged on her gently but firmly, and the stars behind her eyes went completely white.

She rose off the bed, arching into him, shoving her hips into his face as she sought every drop of pleasure. He didn't stop sucking, didn't stop making her come. It lasted far longer than she'd thought it would, her limbs dissolving into nothingness, her blood pounding in her veins, her skin on fire with heat, her voice a raw sound in her throat as she cried out.

And then he was kissing his way up her belly, stopping to shower attention on her nipples again before finding his way to her mouth and taking it in a hot, wet kiss. She tasted herself, but she didn't mind. Her body floated in a sea of satisfaction—and yet she sensed there was more pleasure to come if she had the strength for it.

"My turn," she said when he finally broke the kiss.

"Nah, baby, not this time," he murmured, licking the skin of her throat. "I want to be inside you."

She wanted it too.

"Got to get a condom," he said, rolling away from her and reaching for something. His bag on the floor. A moment later he was back, shorts gone and a foil packet in his hand.

"Let me." She took it from him and ripped it open with surprisingly shaky fingers. What the hell?

He lay back to give her access. She wrapped her hand around him, her gut clenching. Oh my… he was so solid. So big and hard. She rolled the condom down as far as she could, and then she let him go. He didn't move or speak, and neither did she.

Then he reached out and ran the back of his hand against her cheek. "You sure about this, Miranda Jane?"

Her pulse skittered. Her belly tightened. She put a hand on his wrist and ran it up his arm. "I want you, Cody. That hasn't changed in the past few minutes."

"That's good to hear, baby, because I'm aching for you something powerful right now."

Her confidence surged. She pushed him onto his back and straddled him. His broad hands clamped around her hips, gently, as she sat there and stared down at the smooth skin and hard muscle beneath her.

"You're so beautiful," she said and then blushed. What the fuck? She did not do sweet nothings. Not even with Mark—and she'd thought she was in love with him at one time.

"Thanks, honey. But I can't hold a candle to you." He reached up and toyed with her nipples, those sensitive little beasts that tingled and ached anew at his touch. "Love these nipples. So beautiful and responsive."

She'd always hated her nipples. They were too big, too prone to showing through her clothing when she was cold or aroused. But when Cody touched them, she felt like they were indeed special.

"They love you too," she said on a sigh.

He lifted his head and pulled her forward until he could suck one into his mouth. "Mmmm, sweet," he said. "Like the rest of you."

Her juices were dripping down her thighs now. Much more of that and she'd embarrass herself with how wet she was.

He reached between them, his fingers skimming her clit.

"You are so fucking wet," he groaned. "It's a crime you've been celibate—but the caveman in me is pretty damned happy you were. Because I get to be the man who reminds you how awesome sex can be."

"Don't disappoint me," she said hoarsely.

"Not a chance, sunshine. You're gonna melt, baby. Swear it."

She believed him. He gripped his cock then and positioned it beneath her. She didn't need any urging to sink down on him. Her muscles burned in spite of how wet she was, because it had been so long.

And maybe because he was hung. Seriously hung. She sucked in a breath and told herself to relax. But she needn't have worried because Cody circled her clit again and again with his thumb. He didn't move at all, didn't shove himself inside her and pump like his life depended on it.

She had to admit that she'd half feared that, even though he'd been patient enough to take care of her first. Some men were that way. They thought because they got you off that you then didn't care what they did in order to get themselves off.

"You okay?" he asked when he slid all the way home.

She could feel him pulsing inside her. Feel his power and his restraint.

And she suddenly wanted to own that power. Wanted to shatter that restraint.

"Never better," she said as she started to move on him. She went slowly at first, letting her body grow accustomed to him, and then faster as the pressure built deep inside her again.

She threw her head back, curled her nails into his shoulders. He gripped her hips—to steady her or direct her she didn't know—but let her set the pace.

"Oh God," she gasped as the tension inside her tightened almost unbearably. "It's so good… So. Damn. Good…"

He put his thumb right where it bumped against her clit as she bounced up and down on him. She'd thought she could hold out, thought it would take a little longer to reach her climax—but she was wrong.

She shattered with a hoarse cry. She would have collapsed against him, but he flipped her like she was made of feathers, pushing her legs wide and pumping into her in just such a way that he hit the bundle of nerves in her G-spot.

"Keep coming for me, Miranda," he commanded her, never letting up, never tiring as he pressed her into the mattress. The bed squeaked mightily and the headboard rocked against the wall, but she didn't care. All she cared about was the orgasm ripping through her body at that moment.

It was the most intense, the most surprising, sexual experience of her life. Maybe it was the situation and the tension, or maybe it was the man. Whatever it was, her body was on fire with pleasure.

"Cody," she cried out. "Oh fuck, don't stop. Please don't stop."

"As much as you want, baby. I'm here."

She didn't know how long the orgasm lasted, but Cody was good as his word. He pumped into her hard and quick, dragging it out. When she was spent, when he felt the tension in her limbs release, he gave in to his own pleasure, his body stilling as he shoved deep and let go. Only the jerk of his hips and the harshness of his breath in her ear told her he was coming.

When it was over, he kissed her cheek, her neck, then licked her nipple before getting off her and disappearing to take care of the condom.

Miranda stretched happily. Yeah, maybe she'd regret this in the morning, but right now? Hell, right now she was congratulating herself on such a good idea. Now if only she could manage to fall asleep, her night would be perfect.

As if thinking about it made it happen, sleep crashed down on her and she heard no more.

CHAPTER FOURTEEN

"THAT'S BULLSHIT," CODY hissed into the phone. He glanced over his shoulder to make sure he was still alone. He'd awakened an hour ago, feeling more relaxed than he had in a long time. The remnants of the dream had completely faded, and Miranda had been sprawled beside him on her belly, her arm flung over the pillow. He'd wanted to wake her and do a repeat of last night, but the truth was that he wasn't sure she'd agree.

She'd said she knew what she was doing. That she wasn't going to regret the fact they'd fucked when they barely knew each other. In his experience, very few women were wired for one-night stands. They got emotional even when they said they wouldn't.

Instead of waking her, he'd let her sleep and gone outside on the porch to enjoy the early-morning desert air after he'd made a cup of coffee in the Keurig. It had been pretty enjoyable until Viking called him a few minutes ago.

"Sorry, Cowboy," Viking said. "But you have to bring her in. She's not operating on a sanctioned mission. She has a personal beef with Victor Conti—she was going to kill him, not infiltrate his organization."

Cody's stomach churned with anger and denial. "She could have killed him at any point—why try to worm her way into his operations to do it? It doesn't make sense."

Except that she'd carried a gun to her meeting with Conti when she wouldn't carry a phone. A suicide mission? Miranda didn't strike him as suicidal.

Viking blew out a breath. "I know that—but it's not our call. Mendez has been on the phone with high-level contacts half the damn night. She's wanted, Cody. The evidence against her is pretty strong."

"What about this Badger guy? He knows something. What's he saying?"

"We don't know his identity for security reasons—but what he's saying through our contacts is that she's a good agent. He also says she's been different since her mentor, this Mark Reed guy, was killed a few months ago."

"I don't like any of this. We said we'd help her."

"And we will. It's all any of us wants. Bring her in and she'll get the help she needs. Samantha Spencer promised to look after her and keep us informed."

His gut was churning harder now. Samantha Spencer was a CIA agent that HOT worked with quite a bit, and she'd always been completely trustworthy. Hell, she was rumored to be hooking up with the skipper. And Mendez was certainly no fool.

So was Miranda lying? Was she obsessed with Conti? It was possible, sure. And yet Cody didn't see it that way.

If she'd wanted to kill Conti, she could have shot him in the lobby of the Venetian. Yeah, she might have been caught—but if she was truly crazy and hell-bent on revenge, she wouldn't have cared. It was also possible, being a highly trained operative, that she could have gotten away if she'd timed everything just right.

There was also the fact she hadn't shot *him* yet. If all she'd wanted was to kill Conti, she wouldn't have let anything stand in her way. She'd have taken Cody down the first chance she had and then doubled back to her target.

No, there were smarter ways to go about eliminating a high-value target like Conti. And Miranda wasn't stupid. If that had been her goal, she'd have gotten the job done.

"Cowboy?" Viking said when Cody stayed silent.

"When and where?" he asked from behind gritted teeth. Because he couldn't disobey a direct order. It would be treason to do so. How the fuck was he going to get out of this?

"Tonight. Ms. Spencer is flying into Vegas. Take Miss Lockwood to the airport, and Ms. Spencer will take it from there."

"Jesus H. Christ," Cody said. "I don't like this, Viking. It's not right."

"If she was HOT, would you stop Mendez from doing what needed done?"

His temples throbbed with a fresh headache. If Miranda was in the military and a member of HOT, no, he wouldn't stop Mendez from taking care of business. But he knew Mendez. Trusted him. He didn't know Samantha Spencer very well, and he damn sure didn't know the CIA brass who wanted Miranda to turn herself in. All he knew was that Miranda didn't want to go. That she was convinced she'd end up dead if she did.

But maybe that was an act—or maybe she really was in need of help. Christ, what a mess.

"No, I wouldn't."

"Same thing, man. The spooks have their own chain of command just like we do."

He blew out a harsh breath. Golden sunlight spilled over the sand and scrub, making everything seem beautiful and new. Hid the ugliness and unfairness of what he had to do to the woman still sleeping in the bed they'd shared last night. Damn it, he wanted more time with her.

But he wasn't going to get it.

"Yeah, all right. What the fuck am I supposed to tell her?"

"Tell her we're helping her solve her problem."

A buzzing noise sounded near her head. Miranda swatted at it, thinking it was a fly or a mosquito—and then she came fully awake when she realized what it really was. The burner phone sat on the bedside table. Ringing.

It shouldn't be ringing. She'd blocked the number before she called Badger. She snatched it up, considering whether or not she should answer. But curiosity overwhelmed her, and she pressed the button.

"Miranda?" a female voice said. "Are you there?"

"Who wants to know?" She didn't recognize the voice, but clearly the woman knew who she was. And knew the number to call.

"It's Samantha Spencer."

She pulled the phone away from her ear and stared at it for a moment. "How do I know that's true?"

She knew who Samantha Spencer was. She'd been on the Middle East bureau for quite some time, and she was legendary. Then she'd left and presumably returned to Washington. Miranda didn't know that for certain because she wasn't acquainted with Samantha. Mark had known her though.

"I was a friend of Mark Reed's," she said, almost as if reading the direction of Miranda's thoughts. "We worked together several years ago."

"If you were his friend, then tell me his childhood nickname. The one he hated."

"What makes you think we were that close?"

"If you don't know it, I'm hanging up."

There was a sigh on the other end. "Really, darling, you shouldn't go off half-cocked all the time. That's what gets good operatives in trouble. And his nickname was Bubba. Which, yes, he despised. His sister told me at a party once."

Miranda closed her eyes. "What do you want, Ms. Spencer?"

"Call me Sam. Right now that handsome SEAL you're with is being told to bring you in. He's not going to want to do it—but he will in the end."

There was a sharp pain right behind her eyes at that news. Yes, they'd had one hot night together—but they still had jobs to do. Cody wasn't going to risk his career for her—just like she wouldn't risk hers for him if the situation were reversed. A prickle of doubt slid down her spine, but she shook it off.

No, of course she wouldn't risk her career for him. She didn't even know him. Not really.

"Why are you telling me this?"

"Because I need you to understand what I'm about to ask of you."

"If you intend to ask me to harm Cody, I'm not going to do it."

Sam laughed. "Hardly, my dear. It would be a waste not only of a sexy man but of a damned fine Special Operator as well. There aren't enough of them to toss away so casually."

Miranda felt herself grinding her teeth. "Then what?"

"I need you to betray him before he betrays you."

The pain behind her eyes intensified. "And what do you mean by that?"

"I mean that if you want to live, if you want to get out of this mess you've gotten yourself into, then you need to do *exactly* what I tell you to do. No matter how difficult. Understood?"

Miranda's chest ached. For what? For a man she'd known only a few hours? A man she'd had fantastic sex with, sure, but what more was there between them? Nothing, that's what. They were strangers, nothing more. No matter how he'd held her close when she'd been upset over the way her life had imploded. He'd been nothing but kind. Helpful. Loyal.

And yet this was her life. Her career. She couldn't go down without a fight. She had to get the evidence to bring down Conti's organization. It was justice for Mark's life and his sacrifice.

"It's not only you in this mess," Sam said, as if sensing her inner turmoil. "You've dragged Cody into it. He could be in danger too if you don't follow my instructions."

She thought of the man who'd touched her so sweetly last night, and determination filled her. No way could she let him be in danger because of her. "Tell me what you want me to do."

CHAPTER FIFTEEN

WHEN CODY WENT back inside, he heard movement in the bedroom. Miranda was awake. He strode over and pushed the door open. She was standing beside the bed, dragging on her jeans. She stopped in the process of doing so and stared at him.

His chest tightened. God, she was beautiful. And she had no idea what was coming. What he had to do.

"How you doing?" he asked.

She dropped her gaze to the floor. Was that a blush?

"Fine. A little sore."

At the thought of how she'd gotten that way, his cock started to tingle with arousal. *Not now.*

"Sorry about that."

Her whiskey eyes were on his, wide and innocent. "Oh no, I loved it. Really. It's been a long time and you—you treated me right. Thank you."

Fuck.

"You're welcome."

She finished pulling her jeans on and spread her hands. "Look, I don't want this to be awkward, okay? We had sex. I don't expect anything from you. I don't want anything."

Now why did her words make him angry? He got what she was saying, and yet it pissed him off anyway.

"What if I want something?"

Her eyes widened a second. And then she looked… hurt? Regretful? A moment later she masked her expression, and he couldn't tell what it was he'd seen.

"What could you possibly want?"

"Maybe I want to know more about you." Whoa, since when had he ever wanted to know more about a woman he slept with?

She looked uncertain, and he hurried on. No way was he going to sound needy. That was weird. And not at all like him.

"I could also want you to know that I intend to do everything I can to help you, Miranda. I could want you to know that I'm not going to stop until we find out who betrayed you. No matter what happens, I want you to know that."

Because tonight, when he handed her over to Samantha Spencer, she was going to hate him.

Her throat moved as she swallowed. "I appreciate that. You've been more than kind to me."

Now it was his turn to look pained. Goddammit, he still hadn't figured out how he was going to obey orders and keep his promise to her at the same time. But he would. He had no choice.

"I've been on the phone with my guys. We're going to have to head back to Vegas and catch a flight out."

She straightened from where she'd bent to pick up her shoes. "Is that a good idea? Conti could be looking for us. He'll have spies at the airport."

"We're boarding a private plane. Different part of the airport than commercial."

That much was true. Samantha Spencer was flying in on a government jet. He hated to think how much that was costing the taxpayers. Or just why it was necessary.

"All right. When do we go?"

Cody frowned. He hadn't expected her to agree so easily. "We have a few hours. The flight will be tonight, so there's no need to leave just yet."

Miranda sat on the bench at the end of the bed and put on her shoes. Not the heels from yesterday but a pair of tennis shoes with a bright pink stripe down the side.

"I thought I smelled coffee," she said, glancing at him for a second.

"Yep."

"Great. I could use some." She stood and brushed past him, not touching him or looking at him again.

Yeah, so it was awkward. They'd had sex last night, and now there was all the uncomfortable morning-after stuff to deal with. Any other time, any other woman, and he'd get up in the morning and walk away. There might be another session before he did, or he might just slip into his clothes and leave before she woke up.

But he couldn't do that this time, even if he wanted to. Which, strangely, he didn't. Neither of them could walk away right now, and that was fine with him.

"There's bread for toast," he said as he walked out in-to the living room. She glanced at him from the kitchen as she popped a K-Cup into the Keurig. “Might be cereal too. I didn’t check.”

“Great. Thanks.”

He’d eaten an energy bar from the stash in his duffel, so he hadn’t paid a lot of attention to what the safe house was stocked with. Miranda fixed her coffee and then poked around in the cabinets. She found cereal, poured a bowl, and ate it standing over the sink in the kitchen, staring out the window.

He wanted to know what she was thinking, but he wouldn’t ask. He also had an urge to walk over and slip his arms around her, tug her into his embrace. He wasn’t going to do that either.

She finished the cereal and rinsed her bowl. But she still didn’t leave the window. She stood there drinking her coffee, watching the road. It was empty of traffic, a dusty ribbon winding from the main road to the safe house, which sat tucked away in the scrub.

If he looked out the east window, he could see another house about a mile away. It was sparsely populated out here. Not many people wanted to live in the desert, he supposed. Or at least not in this part of the desert.

Cody went out to the truck, stashed his duffel inside, and checked his weapon. His team had made sure he had one when they’d gotten the truck for him last night. The gun was a 9mm, not as sweet as his Sig, but it would get the job done.

He shut the door and was turning to go back inside when a cloud of dust caught his eye. It was near the beginning of the road leading down to the house. There was no need for anyone to come down that road, but someone could be turning around.

And yet the cloud kept moving toward him, swirling around a black SUV that barreled along the road.

Cody sprinted to the door and threw it open. "Miranda! We've got company! Get your shit and get out here. *Now!*"

He started the truck with the remote key fob and turned impatiently, looking for Miranda. She came running out the door, gun drawn. They ran for the truck and jumped inside, doors slamming.

He jammed it into reverse, rammed his foot on the gas, and rocketed backward. Then he executed a one-eighty and cranked the truck into drive. The only way out was the road the SUV approached on. Yeah, this was the desert and the terrain was flat, but it was rocky too. He wasn't taking the chance of bottoming out the truck, piercing the gas tank, or damaging the transmission and turning them into sitting ducks. The only thing to do was fly toward the SUV and play chicken.

Miranda propped a foot onto the glove compartment to steady herself, grabbed the handle above the door for support, and aimed the pistol over her knee. Cody shot her a look, his chest swelling with emotions he didn't understand or have time to analyze.

But goddamn, she was spectacular. Tough and beautiful and deadly all at once. He'd never known that kind of thing could be a turn-on, but holy fuck, it sure was. He'd dated military women in the past, so he was used to tough-as-nails females, but none of them had been quite like Miranda.

She was cut from the same cloth as he was, and he liked it more than he'd ever thought possible. Her long hair hung over her shoulders, and her jaw was set at a determined angle. When they got out of this, he was looking forward to kissing her again, to watching that jaw soften as he brought her pleasure.

"I don't know how they found us, but we got this, sunshine," he said coolly. "I promise."

She glanced at him, her whiskey eyes looking haunted. "We don't even know who they are," she said. "Conti? Or the agency? Or maybe it's your guys deciding they don't want to help me after all."

That last statement pierced his conscience in ways he didn't like. "Does it matter who they are?"

Her eyes hardened. "No."

They flew down the road toward the SUV. Miranda kept aim, and Cody prepared to perform evasive maneuvers. The SUV grew bigger, the headlights shining through the dust. The driver wasn't wavering yet—but he would.

Cody mashed the gas harder, and the truck responded with a surge of power, rocks spitting and plinking against the sides—

And then the truck died. Just fucking died. All the power went away as the brakes locked up and they skidded over the dirt. Cody held the wheel hard, keeping the truck straight as they slid. They came to a stop and his stomach twisted as he reached for the key and turned it again and again. Nothing happened. Nothing.

"Fuck!" He slammed his palm against the steering wheel and then grabbed his gun as he flung the door open. He didn't know how, but they'd disabled the truck remotely.

"Follow me," he ordered Miranda as he tumbled out and took up position behind the tires. He wasn't giving up yet. No fucking way.

He heard Miranda fall to the dirt. And then he felt her behind him, one hand lightly stroking over his shoulders. "It's okay," she said softly, her breath tickling the shell of his ear as she leaned in and kissed his cheek. "It's over, Cody. You tried."

Before he knew what she intended, she stood and walked out in front of the truck. Her gun hung limply at her side.

"Goddammit, Miranda," he shouted. "Get down."

She didn't move as the SUV rolled up. And then her arm came up, aiming at the vehicle. Cody started to go after her and drag her down, but a shot rang out and then another—

Miranda dropped like a stone in the dirt, her golden hair billowing over the rocks and scrub as she fell. Cody roared with rage as he surged upright, intending to shoot every last motherfucker in that vehicle. He prayed she was only hit, not dead, but his brain knew better. They'd been too close, the aim too precise. There was blood everywhere, her blood…

"Drop it, sailor. That's an order." Samantha Spencer sat in the passenger seat, window down, staring at him. But it was the semiautomatic rifle aimed at him from the rear passenger seat that made him check himself.

"What the fuck have you done?" he demanded, rage boiling inside him. Miranda's body was still, her face turned away from him. Blood spattered her shirt and pooled beneath her body, soaking the sand. It made him ill in a way that blood and bodies never had before. At least they hadn't shot her with the semi or she'd have been torn to pieces.

He started toward her but the gun in the window jerked and Samantha growled. "Stand down and drop your weapon."

Cody complied, his stomach twisting. He didn't look at Miranda again. He couldn't. Samantha held his gaze.

"We did what was necessary. Now get back in your truck and drive away."

"I was bringing her to you tonight. Why the fuck did you shoot her? Why not just wait for me to bring her to you?"

Samantha's gaze never wavered. "She was dangerous. *You* were in danger, whether you realize it or not. She would have killed you rather than let you bring her in. Now drive away and forget about this."

"You didn't have to shoot her," he insisted, his gut churning with fury and nausea. He'd been inside her last night. She'd been alive beneath him. So alive and beautiful. Dangerous? No fucking way. Not like that.

"She shot at us first. It's regrettable, but it's done. Get in your truck and drive. *Now.* That's a direct order, sailor. Disobey me and you'll be answering to Colonel Mendez."

As if on cue, his phone rang. He answered with a clipped, "McCormick."

"Drive away, son." It was Mendez's voice. "Let the CIA handle the situation."

That was the moment when he knew it was over. The end. Nothing more he could do. *Goddammit!*

"Yes, sir," he said, his heart aching. He didn't want to accept the truth, but he had no choice. Miranda was dead. He'd promised to help her, and he'd failed spectacularly. He'd let her down, and she'd paid with her life.

He got in the truck and turned the key, his body on autopilot. He was numb. He couldn't feel a damned thing. Couldn't process everything that had happened.

The truck started as if nothing had ever gone wrong. As if this had merely been a bad dream and not reality. He put it into gear and backed away. The last thing he saw in the rearview was two men get out of the SUV and pick up Miranda's lifeless body.

He put the pedal down and drove.

Miranda didn't move until she was placed into the SUV. Then she sat up and pulled her shirt away from her body. The blood from the capsules they'd fired at her was sticky and messy. Someone handed her a towel, and she pressed it to her body.

"Sorry about that," Sam said from the front seat. She knew it was Sam because it was the same voice from the phone call.

Miranda's throat was tight. Her eyes stung. Now why on earth was she so upset over the fact she'd had to lie to a man she'd known for less than twenty-four hours? He'd been on her side, sure, but she'd had to do it. For his sake and hers. Or so she'd been told.

"I don't know why we had to do it that way," she grated. "It could have all gone wrong so quickly."

"Yes, but it didn't. I know the HOT boys. I know how they're trained."

"He could have been told what was happening," she said, guilt suffusing her. "We didn't need to stage a deception like this."

Sam's eyes were sharp as she turned to look at Miranda over the seat. "You needed to die, Miranda. The fewer people who know the truth, the better. There's a mole in the agency, and we need to find out who it is. I can't have a military Special Operator, a HOT operator—someone I do not control—knowing you're alive. I told you he could be in danger too. Do you even care about that?"

Miranda swallowed. Of course she did. But it was too easy to think of Cody as being invincible. Strong and trustworthy. Someone she wanted in her corner.

"Besides," Sam continued, "it's bad enough we had to do it the way we did. He knows it was me, and I'd rather that wasn't the case. I'd rather he think Victor Conti got to you—but there wasn't enough time to set that up. If he were anyone other than HOT, neutralizing him wouldn't have been an issue."

She knew what Sam meant. Cody was highly trained and deadly. If he'd thought they were Conti's men, he'd have killed them—or at least one of them before he'd been stopped. And how would they have stopped him? A tranquilizer? That would have been a dead giveaway when he woke up. Because Conti's men would have killed him, not put him to sleep.

No, he had to know it was the agency who'd killed her because he had to be ordered to stand down. And he had to be willing to accept the order, which is why he needed to see Sam's face.

Miranda ran a shaky hand through her hair. It was tangled and dirty now, but she didn't care. She could still hear Cody's rage. Still feel the sickening emotion in the pit of her stomach as she lay there and pretended to be dead. She'd had to fall just right, with her back angled to the tire opposite so he couldn't see the absence of a gaping exit wound. And she couldn't lie completely on her back because then he'd see her breathe. It had been tricky, but he'd been pissed and the situation had been confusing, which was what they'd counted on.

And yet it felt all wrong to lie to him like that, to cut him out of the loop so suddenly and violently. But she'd had no choice. Not if she wanted her life back. And not if she wanted to protect him from whoever was after her.

Tears sprang to her eyes and she dashed them away angrily. What the hell? She was an agent, a trained operative. She did what was necessary. Did the dirty work. She did not feel regret for doing the job.

Not until today anyway.

"You heard him. He had orders to take you in. Did you forget that?"

Yes, she'd heard him, and she'd felt his betrayal like a blow. It didn't make her feel any less guilty for what she'd done though. "No, I didn't forget."

"He would have obeyed those orders, same as you obeyed yours." Sam reached back and patted her arm. "We've got work to do. Are you ready to do it?"

Miranda gritted her teeth and swallowed down the uncharacteristic emotion boiling inside her. It made no sense why she was upset about this. Cody was a nice guy, but she didn't care about him. She couldn't.

Liar.

"Yes," she said, shoving away the voice in her head. The emotion. The regret for what she'd done. She was a machine. An operative with a job to do. She didn't have room for softness or tender feelings in her life. "Yes, I'm ready. Let's do this thing."

CHAPTER SIXTEEN

Six weeks later...

HE'D SEEN DEATH before. Many times. Hell, he'd been the instrument of death more times than he liked to think about. Death was not a surprise to him.

And yet Miranda Lockwood's death still haunted him. Cody took a swig of his beer and watched the guys playing pool. They were at Buddy's tonight, the team having returned from a mission just a week ago. It had been a quick in and out, and now they were back. He would have liked the mission to last longer. To be more distracting.

But it hadn't been, and he was still thinking about Miranda's golden hair and whiskey eyes. About the way she'd sighed and moaned when he'd been inside her, taking them both to nirvana. Jesus, being inside her had been exciting. Being with her had been exciting.

And now she was gone. Her life snuffed out on the side of an Arizona desert road. What the fuck did it all mean?

"You playing, dude, or what?" It was Cage looking at

him. Cage, who was a shark at pool even though he didn't look it. Cody knew better than to bet money against Cage when it came to a game. Cage was busy taking out the members of HOT's Echo Squad since they hadn't gotten fully acquainted with his sharkiness yet. Alpha Squad knew better already. The SEALs definitely knew better.

Cody tipped up his beer again. "Nope. Just watching you fleece our teammates."

Cage grinned. One of the Echo guys was lining up a shot as Cage came over and leaned against the tall table Cody sat at. "Not fleecing. I'm a married man now. Have to put away money for the missus and me."

Cody snorted. "Dude, your wife is part owner of an oil company. You don't need the money."

Cage shrugged. "You never know, man. Rainy days and all that, *mon ami*."

Yeah, you damn well never knew. Never knew that the woman who abducted you in broad daylight would be dead twenty-four hours later no matter how hard you tried to protect her. Never knew how empty and cold that would make you feel or how you wouldn't be able to stop thinking about it. How it would wake you up in the middle of the night, your body covered in sweat and your throat raw from the screaming you'd done.

Whatever he'd dreamed about before Miranda, it was nothing compared to what he dreamed about *after* Miranda.

"Hey, you okay, Cowboy?"

Cody met Cage's gaze. His teammate was looking at him quizzically. "Yeah, fine. Why?"

Cage blew out a breath. "You haven't been yourself since Vegas."

His insides crystallized into ice. "I'm fine. It's nothing we haven't encountered many times before."

"Yeah, except she was shot on your watch."

Cody shrugged. "She was dangerous. A loose cannon."

Cage's gaze sharpened. "You don't believe that."

There was a lump in Cody's throat. A fucking lump. "No, I really don't. I know the CIA thought so. I know the skipper thought so. I guess they know more than I do. But I still can't wrap my head around it. She could have killed me if she'd wanted. Killed me and taken the truck. She didn't. They haven't fucking explained that one to me yet."

He'd driven back to Vegas that day, as directed, his heart throbbing and his gut aching the entire time. He'd replayed the scene over and over again. What the fuck had possessed Miranda to step out in front of the truck the way she had? She was a fighter, not a quitter. He knew that much about her after one night together.

But then she'd said to him as she'd kissed his cheek that it was over, that he'd tried. Before he knew what she was about, she'd stepped into the open.

She'd fucking quit. Why? It didn't add up in his head.

He'd gone into autopilot mode as he'd driven across the desert. He'd found Maggie at the Bellagio, draped over the arm of a high roller. A married man by the looks of the ring on his finger. Cody had sobered her up and returned her to his grandparents even though they all knew she'd take off again. He'd spent a few days herding cattle on the ranch to clear his head, then went back to Vegas and watched Cage marry Christina with Elvis officiating. It had been over the top, but not tacky. The SEALs were all there, as well as most of Alpha Squad.

He'd tried to be happy for Cage, but he kept seeing Miranda sprawled in the dirt, blood seeping from her body. They hadn't even let him check her for vitals.

As if there would have been any. As if he could have saved her.

Returning to DC hadn't been any easier. Mendez called him in the moment he was back. The skipper was a tough man to read, but there was sympathy and even anger in his gaze when Cody went into his office. He hadn't understood the anger at all. Still didn't.

"I'm sorry it went down that way," Mendez said. "I did what I could do. It wasn't enough."

"I know you tried, sir. Thank you."

"This situation turned out to be bigger than HOT's mandate. I had to cooperate with the CIA on this one. The result was not what I wanted."

"I appreciate your help, sir."

And that was the end of that. Well, other than a visit to the shrink. Just like coming home from any other mission, there was a mandatory debrief. The only thing that wasn't like other missions was the debrief with the CIA. It took everything he had not to lose his shit with those guys—but Samantha Spencer wasn't there, which was the only thing that prevented it. If she'd strolled in— Well, it wouldn't have ended well for him, that was for certain. There were things he wanted to know, and Samantha was the one with the answers.

The agents sent to question him were very thorough, asking for every last detail of his time with Miranda. He gave them the facts and nothing else. Then they wanted to know about her death. He gave the information to them coldly and matter-of-factly, burning with anger as he did so. When he finished, he stood and snapped to attention before walking out and leaving them with their pens and notepads. They hadn't dismissed him, but he'd gone anyway.

They had not called him back.

A week later, the SEALs were on a mission and Miranda settled to the back of his brain. She never went away, no matter what he did.

Of all he'd seen and done, she haunted him quite possibly the most. Why?

Cage tapped his stick against the floor, jarring Cody from his thoughts. "Maybe she had another plan," he said, and Cody had to think for a second.

Oh, right. They'd been talking about the fact that Miranda hadn't killed him when she'd had the chance. "Could be," he replied. Because what else was he supposed to say? That she wasn't a rogue agent, that she'd tasted fucking amazing, and that she'd screamed so sweetly when he'd taken her to orgasm again and again?

Cage gripped his shoulder and gave him a friendly squeeze. "I'm on your side, buddy. Swear to God. If you say she wasn't going to kill you, I believe it. But it doesn't matter anymore, yeah? She's gone and she ain't coming back."

Cody didn't answer because he didn't need to.

"Hey, *mon ami*," Cage called to the Echo Squad guy, moving toward the pool table. "You ready to lose?"

"Cocky, aren't you? I missed one ball. There are a lot left to sink."

Cage laughed. "Yeah, man. That's me. Cocky to a fault. Watch and weep, baby," he said as he bent over the table and lined up the shot.

Cody glanced over at the television hanging above the bar. Buddy kept it on a news channel most of the time, and tonight was no exception. But the headline scrolling across the bottom caught Cody's attention.

Victor Conti Flees US Ahead of Alleged Arrest Warrant

Ice settled in Cody's belly. Jesus. Not only was Miranda dead, but Victor-fucking-Conti wasn't even going to be held accountable for any of his crimes. He'd gotten away with everything and paid nothing. Miranda had gotten away with nothing and paid everything.

It wasn't fucking fair.

Cody signaled the waitress and ordered another beer. He had a feeling he was going to need a few more before the night was through.

"Man, you need me to go in with you?"

Cody turned his head to look at Cash "Money" McQuaid. His teammate was a little blurry, but not too bad. Yeah, he'd had a few, and yeah, he'd had to leave his car behind and let Cash bring him home. He'd get his car in the morning when Cash swung by and picked him up again.

Provided his head hadn't cracked open by then. He sure knew enough about the mechanics of a hangover, thanks to Maggie, to know what was coming. Not that he hadn't had one or two himself, but he generally avoided them. Growing up with a mother who needed you to hold her hair while she puked and then asked you to bring her aspirin and a sports drink in the morning when her head was pounding sort of knocked the desire for overindulgence right out of a fella.

Except for tonight apparently.

"Nah, I'll be fine. Just get me tomorrow. Eight sharp."

Money laughed. "I kinda doubt that, Cowboy. Good thing we're still on leave or your ass would be hurting if you had to report to Mendez at 0600."

"Yeah, whatever. Call me. I'll be ready."

Money looked at him with more sympathy than Cody liked. Dammit, did everybody think he was still broken up over the Miranda thing?

"You've had a rough few weeks. It's understandable you'd want to tie one on. I think you can take the time to recover properly. How about you call me tomorrow when you're ready? I'll come get you."

Cody fumbled for the door handle. He just wanted to get inside and lie down. Forget things for a while. "Fine. I'll call you."

The door opened and he stepped onto the pavement. The ground wobbled a little, but it was mostly okay. He shut the door and started up the sidewalk, reaching into his jeans pocket for his keys. His apartment was on the third floor, and he had to walk up the central stairwell to get to it since there was no elevator. He normally didn't think twice about it, but tonight he sure wished he didn't have to go so far.

He started up the steps, holding on to the railing as

much to steady himself as to guide his steps. Once he reached the top landing, he only had to turn left and his door was right there. First he had to get to the top though.

He made it up to the first landing and turned. The light was out at the second landing, but it had been that way since before he'd gone on the last mission. He made a mental note to call the super or change the damn thing himself.

Cody started up the next set of steps, the beer sloshing in his belly more than he would like. Dammit, this was why he didn't overindulge. Why he normally had more control. It was all because of Miranda. His life had been different since that day in the desert, and he didn't like it one bit.

He reached the top of the next landing—and a man stepped out of the shadow of a doorway, startling him. That pissed him off because his senses were usually better than that. He relied on them to keep him alive out in the field, and now he couldn't even tell there was a guy on the landing?

Good thing this wasn't an op.

"Hey, man," he said by way of friendly greeting.

"Hey, yourself," the guy said. And then something jammed into Cody's ribs from behind.

"What the—?" he said, starting to turn.

"Don't move, asshole," a guy's voice growled.

The beer wasn't helping matters, but Cody had enough training and determination to center his thoughts and focus in a way he hadn't been able to only a moment before.

"What do you want? My wallet? It's in my back pocket."

"No, we don't want your wallet," the guy in front of him said. "You're coming with us—and you're doing it quietly."

"All right." He wasn't going quietly, but damned if he was telling them that. He still had his keys in his hand, and he shifted them around until he had one sticking between his fingers like a weapon. *Think, Cody.*

"Care to tell me what this is about?"

The guy behind him snorted. "Mr. Conti wishes to speak to you."

Cody blinked. "Wow, really? I thought he left the country."

"Which is why you're leaving too."

"Damn, I'd love to help, but I really can't do that, fellas."

"You don't have a choice, asshole."

"I think I do." He'd been trained in a hell these guys couldn't imagine to react precisely the way he did. He let years of conditioning take over. Without thinking about it, he disarmed the guy behind him in one swift move and then pivoted to shove the key into the guy's throat. A second later as the other guy moved in, Cody kicked the man's knees from beneath him and then disabled him with a sharp blow to the neck.

"Jesus, what the fuck?" It was Money's voice. Cody looked up to see his teammate's gaze flicking between the two men on the landing.

"Hey, Money. What brings you here?"

"You left your phone in my car. I had to turn around and bring it back. Now what the fuck is this?"

Cody nodded toward the guys on the ground. "Think they're friends of Victor Conti's."

"Aw, hell." Money pulled out his phone. "That means we have to call Viking—and he's gonna call Mendez."

Cody shrugged. He was too far gone to care. "Better call an ambulance too. I might have cut this one's jugular."

CHAPTER SEVENTEEN

"YOU HAVE GOT to be fucking kidding me," Mendez swore.

Alex "Ghost" Bishop watched the CO pace back and forth in one of HOT's ready rooms. They'd both been called back to work in the middle of the night, and Mendez was plenty pissed. Not about being called in, but about the situation.

The SEALs were in another room, and Cowboy was half-plastered. But the dude had fought off two attackers and managed to neutralize them in that condition. Too bad the dumb bastards hadn't realized they'd been sent to grab a Navy SEAL. If they had, maybe they'd have done it differently.

Like maybe they'd have brought six more guys to do the job—and even then Alex figured the odds still wouldn't have been in their favor.

"Victor Conti is attacking my SEALs? How is this possible? How the fuck did he find Cody McCormick in the first place?"

The other end of the phone was silent for a long moment. And then Samantha Spencer's voice came through the speaker of the secure phone. She sounded cool, calm—and annoyed. Alex wasn't sure, but he thought there was an extra level of tension between her and his boss.

"He must have tracked him down from the casino security tapes."

There was another way and they all knew it. But Samantha wasn't going to admit that her inability to find a mole could have led to this situation.

And Mendez wasn't going to let her get away with it.

"Assuming it wasn't your goddamn mole who betrayed my guy, your people were supposed to take care of those tapes," Mendez growled. "You promised that my SEAL would be protected—and I agreed to go along with your fucking death scene in exchange for that promise."

"It had to be done that way," Samantha snapped. "It was the only way to smoke out our mole. If he—or she—thinks Agent Lockwood is dead, they might act a little more recklessly."

They'd all agreed at the time that it was best if Cody wasn't aware the Lockwood girl was alive, but it had been a damned dirty thing to do. Alex hadn't liked it. Mendez hadn't either. But they'd gone along with the CIA because that's what they'd wanted. What they'd insisted upon.

Alex was pretty certain Mendez was done going along with Samantha's ideas.

"And have they acted recklessly? Or are you as clueless to this mole's identity as ever?"

"We're working on it."

"How do you know this traitor didn't give Conti the

information on my SEAL?" Mendez snapped. "Because I could believe that a whole lot easier than I can believe the fucking CIA forgot to erase some tapes."

Alex could practically hear Samantha's teeth grinding together. "No, we don't know who it is or if they're the one who passed the information about your SEAL. But we're close—and we *do* know he or she gave Conti the information that we were coming for him."

"And were you? Or was that just a ruse to get him to run?"

"I can't comment on operations, Colonel. I think you know that."

Mendez looked ready to punch something. "Listen here—you've put one of my operators at risk, which puts HOT at risk. And *that*, Miz Spencer, is a problem."

Samantha sighed. "Look, I don't know what happened—those tapes were destroyed within days, though it's possible Conti got to them first. Access to the files on Miranda Lockwood, including the interview with your SEAL, was supposed to be controlled."

"Then you need to be looking at everyone who had access to those files, don't you?"

"It's going to take time." She was silent for a moment. "We fucked up. Is that what you want me to say?"

Mendez's jaw tightened. "It doesn't fix the problem."

"We know where Conti's gone. We'll get him before he can do more damage. Once we have him, we'll find out who's been giving him inside information."

"And in the meantime, what? I kill my guy too? Give him a new identity?"

"Send him to the sandbox, for Christ's sake! You're a black-ops outfit—put him to work and we'll finish this thing. By the time he gets back, everything will be fine."

Mendez clenched his hands into fists as if he was trying to get hold of his temper. And then he dropped into a chair, propped his feet on the table, and put his hands behind his head. Alex never failed to admire how Mendez could go from pissed to calm in a heartbeat.

Except he knew that the calm was the worst part of all. Samantha Spencer had stepped on a land mine and didn't even know it.

"Tell you what, Agent Spencer—"

Oh fuck, she'd *really* stepped in it now.

"—since you seem to need competent help over there at the CIA, I'm going to do you a favor. I'm going to send my SEALs to finish the job."

Samantha scoffed, but she didn't sound amused. "Thanks, but no. We've got this. You don't even know where Conti is. We do, and it's a delicate situation."

Mendez flipped open the file folder lying on the table in front of him. "Oh yeah, it's delicate all right. Zain Okonjo mean anything to you?"

There was silence for a long moment. "Should it?"

Mendez snorted. "Cut the crap, Sam. Zain Okonjo is the military dictator who overturned the government of Jorwani six months ago."

"I know that. But what's Okonjo got to do with Conti? With anything?"

Mendez's eyes narrowed. "You're really going to make me say it?"

Samantha let out a long breath, acknowledging defeat. "Fine. No, I'm not. But you tell me what you know, and I'll tell you if you're right."

Mendez's laugh was sudden and sharp. But he wasn't

amused. Anyone who made that mistake would pay a price for it.

"I'll tell you this—your boy is under his protection, quite possibly living in his presidential palace, and you don't have the first fucking clue how to get him out of there. We do."

"Jesus Christ," Samantha muttered. "You're an arrogant son of a bitch, Johnny—you know that?"

"Not arrogant. Certain of my boys and their abilities. You want Conti? You need HOT."

"I'd refuse, but I have a feeling you aren't going to let me."

"No, I'm not. And if you try to stonewall me on this, I'm calling in a few favors on the Hill. One way or the other, I will get what I want."

From anyone else, it would sound like arrogance. But Alex knew that Mendez meant what he said. And since the CO had a damned good track record of getting what he wanted, Alex wasn't about to doubt him.

"Fine," Samantha grumbled. "But you're taking one of my operatives with you. I want someone I trust on the inside."

"You don't trust me?"

"Not as far as I can throw you."

"What do you think I'm planning to do? Grab Conti and turn him over to the FBI once I've got him Stateside?"

"Maybe. Maybe you're just pissed enough to do it. And that won't suit us at all. We need him—for his informant's identity, if for nothing else."

"You think he'll tell you the truth?"

"Depends on the incentive, doesn't it?"

She let that hang there, and Alex was sure Mendez

must have imagined the same things he did. Immunity. A plea bargain. A deal of some kind—a country club prison sentence, perhaps?

All the things a man like Conti didn't deserve. Unfortunately, that wasn't the way the world worked sometimes. Every one of those things was a distinct possibility, depending on the CIA's desire for information.

Mendez chewed the inside of his lip. "My SEALs are highly trained. They aren't inserting into Jorwani with a tourist tagging along for the ride."

"First of all, my agents aren't tourists. And secondly, the United States can't officially send *anyone* into Jorwani, and you know it. If your SEALs are going, they'll have to go as mercenaries. Which means no American military transport dropping them into the zone. Not even a destroyer. They'll have to cross the border as civilians."

"Not my first rodeo, Agent Spencer. I've got this."

"Fine. Then you'll take my agent with you, and we'll get everyone out when it's time."

Alex knew she was talking about the secret CIA flights that masqueraded as commercial airliners. HOT didn't have that because they were military and used military transport. Unless the CIA gave them a ride, which often happened depending on the job. Though Alex figured it wasn't going to happen this time—unless Mendez agreed to take the CIA agent along.

"If you insist."

"I do."

Mendez picked up a pen lying on the desk and flicked it open and closed, open and closed. "Send her over quick. We're bugging out in twenty-four hours."

"What makes you think the agent is female?"

Mendez snorted. "Because I know you. You're sending Miranda Lockwood. Is that going to cause trouble for me? Yeah, probably, which is part of the reason you're doing it. But no matter what, I'm telling McCormick the truth now. If you don't like that, then too bad. I'm done going along with your schemes. You've proven to me that it didn't matter one bit whether or not Cody knew the truth in the first place. You've had time to get your mole, and all you've managed to do is lose your high-value target instead."

Alex could practically hear the frost over the phone. "I needed an unimpeachable witness to her death. He fit the bill, and he convinced those who needed to be convinced that it wasn't a ruse. I won't apologize for protecting my agent. And while it's inconvenient for us both that she's going on this mission, I don't have many people on the inside of this operation. She's the only one I *can* send. Unless I want to read in another agent—and I don't want to take the risk. Exposing this operation any wider than it is will only make it harder to complete." She paused, and Alex could tell by the slight crackling sound that she was sucking on her e-cigarette. A moment later, she blew out a breath. "Agent Lockwood is dead to the world, and that's what I need. I trust your guy not to fuck her story up."

"He won't. But he could have done the job without the deceit in the first place, Sam. That's what you never seemed to get."

"It was safer for everyone. He was nearly grabbed tonight—what if they'd succeeded? He could have spilled the truth about my agent if they tortured him enough. And then what? Conti would know she was alive, and he'd tell his informant—who would go underground so deep we'd never find the leak."

Mendez rocked back in his chair. "You really have no idea what my guys are capable of, do you?"

"He's human. He has a breaking point."

"I'm beginning to think you don't understand HOT at all. Or me."

Alex wasn't sure why he added that last part, but it seemed to have the effect of silencing Samantha for a few moments.

"I do the best I can with the information I have. I work with facts, not faith."

Mendez sat up again, his finger hovering over the disconnect button. "Twenty-four hours. She better be ready to go."

He disconnected before Samantha could reply. And then he looked at Alex for the first time since the conversation had begun. There was a hint of anger in those dark eyes, and something more besides. But Alex knew he wasn't going to find out what any of it meant.

"When McCormick sobers up, I want to see him."

"Yes, sir," Alex replied before getting to his feet and retreating.

Miranda put on her sunglasses even though it wasn't all that bright yet. Dawn had crept into the sky a couple of hours earlier, but there were clouds that morning. She climbed into the back seat of the Town Car sent to fetch her. Sam waited inside, looking up from her government-issued Blackberry the moment Miranda sat down.

"You ready for this?" she asked as the car started to move. There were no preambles with Sam. Straight to the point and that was it.

But Miranda had been born ready, so she answered the only way she could. "I am."

She was also tired of waiting. Tired of sitting around and hoping the traitor in the CIA would make a wrong move. Since she'd been declared dead, she'd been waiting for that to happen. It hadn't. She'd somehow thought she'd barrel right back into the agency and help smoke out this person, but of course that wasn't the way it worked.

She'd gotten a new name, a new hair color and cut, new contacts to change the color of her eyes. She was Jane Wood these days. Sam had asked her back in Arizona, when she was still sticky with fake blood, if she was ready to do the work to catch a mole. She'd said yes—and then she'd been sent to Luxembourg where she'd spent a month doing nothing but following the money trail Victor Conti left in his wake. It had been important work because it had led them to Jorwani, but it still hadn't gotten them anywhere closer to tracking down the leak in the agency. Two weeks ago, she'd returned to DC to wait further instruction.

Now Victor had fled the country and they were no closer to catching the mole. Whoever it was had managed to warn him without leaving a trail. It was almost enough to make a girl lose faith that justice would ever be served or that she would ever get her life back.

Until last night when Sam had called her and told her she was about to work with HOT. Her heart had lodged in her throat. Because HOT meant Cody. And Cody meant a whole range of feelings she hadn't yet managed to sort out.

She'd thought about him a lot over the past six weeks. She'd caught herself thinking about how he'd touched her, about how good she'd felt with him. About how much she'd trusted him. It had been a shock to think back on it, but she really had trusted him with her life.

And then she'd betrayed him by pretending to die. She'd done it because she'd believed she was protecting him. When Sam had told her he might be in danger too, well, she'd swallowed her doubts and done what she was told. She'd had a lot of regrets in the weeks since, but it was too late to fix it.

She'd often wondered how he'd taken her death. Had he shrugged and moved on because that's what he did? Or did he blame himself for not protecting her well enough?

And what was he going to think when he saw her again today? That was the worst of all, the part that she kept trying to imagine and couldn't. What would she say to him? Would he be pissed?

Probably, but dammit, she could be pissed too if she wanted to be. Because he'd been planning to take her in—she'd heard it from his own mouth as she'd lain there in the dirt—and he wouldn't have told her he was doing it. He'd have obeyed orders just like she had.

However you sliced it, her day was about to get really damned awkward.

Sam handed her an envelope. Inside was a Canadian passport for Jane Wood. A fake, of course, but a good one.

"You'll need this to get into Jorwani. The Canadians are still sending aid, and Okonjo is still allowing them access."

"Why are you sending me?" That was the thing that had been puzzling her since Sam called last night. They'd gone to a lot of trouble to fake her death and make Cody believe it. And now it was about to be undone. Oh, she'd still be dead to the world—but not to Cody. As Sam had pointed out once before, the CIA didn't control Cody. But maybe Sam trusted the person who did. Whatever the case, Miranda was about to come back to life for someone who believed her dead.

Sam sighed and pressed her lips together. "The truth?"

"Yes."

Her shoulders lifted in a half shrug. "You're expendable, Jane. You're already dead, and if anything goes wrong and you're caught— Well, we have deniability."

It was brutal, sure, but it also made sense. "Then I'll do my best not to get caught."

Sam grinned. "I sure hope so. I want Victor Conti's balls on a spit, and then I want whoever this bastard is who compromised us. I want justice for Mark Reed as much as you do."

"Not quite as much as I do," Miranda said. Because if Sam had wanted justice eight months ago, Miranda had no doubt it would have happened by now.

Sam spread her hands. "All right, not as much. But I still want it. I don't like losing good agents—and I really don't like it when it's so fucking senseless." She looked at her phone. "We don't have a lot of time before we arrive, and there are still a few things you need to know about where you're going and who you'll see."

Sam didn't stop talking until they reached the plain building sitting behind yards of razor wire. The car drew to a halt, but the engine didn't stop. Two military guards in uniform stood by the gate to the compound, M16s resting across their chests. Miranda turned to Sam as the driver got out and went around to the trunk where he fetched her small rolling suitcase.

"You aren't going in?" Miranda asked.

Sam shook her head. "Best if the colonel and I don't meet right now," she said. "Good luck, Agent Wood. You couldn't be in better hands than with HOT. I look forward to your return from a successful mission."

"I won't let you down. I want that son of a bitch too much."

Her smile was soft. "I know you do. Now go—and watch yourself with those HOT men. They have a way of getting under a woman's skin."

As if Miranda didn't already know it. She climbed from the car and faced the guards, her belly churning with anticipation. They didn't betray any emotions as they stared stony-faced into the distance. And then one of them looked at her.

"Please come with us, Agent Wood."

Miranda stepped through the gate behind the guard who'd spoken. The other guard fell into position on her heels. The metal clanged shut and a chill slipped through her as if she'd entered a lion's den and couldn't escape.

Too late to back out now. The only way forward was through.

CHAPTER EIGHTEEN

IT TOOK ALMOST fifteen minutes to pass through the layers of security, but finally Miranda was shown to an office with two men who stood when she entered. One was tall and handsome with salt-and-pepper hair and a fierce expression. The other was also tall and handsome, but somehow friendlier looking.

She would know which was which even without the name tapes on their uniforms because Sam had briefed her about Mendez. She hadn't been wrong. The man was the epitome of the word badass. Not the sort you'd want to cross, that's for sure. No wonder Sam had declined to come inside.

"Agent Wood," Colonel Mendez said, reaching out to shake her hand. He didn't squeeze it like he would a man's hand, and for that she was thankful. What was it with men who thought they had to squeeze the daylights out of a woman's hand, anyway?

"Colonel," she replied. She knew they knew her real

name, but clearly they'd decided to go with her cover identity. She could roll with that.

The other man also shook her hand. "Welcome, Agent Wood. I'm Alex Bishop."

"Thank you, Colonel," she said, because even though this man was a lieutenant colonel, technically a rank below Mendez, the appropriate form of address in an informal situation was still colonel. She'd learned that working with the military in foreign embassies and bases around the world.

Mendez sat on one of the chairs arranged around a coffee table, and Lieutenant Colonel Bishop followed suit. Which meant she did as well.

Her heart thumped a bit, not because she was scared, but because she kept thinking about the moment she had to face Cody again. They would have told him she was alive, of course, which meant he'd had some time to think about it by now. But what was he thinking?

"I'm not going to prevaricate with you, Agent Wood. I don't want you on this mission. But Ms. Spencer seems to think you need to be here, so here you are. You need to know, however, that you *will* obey orders as if you're an active-duty soldier assigned to this organization. Any failure to comply and you'll be sitting out the mission on the forward base we launch from. Is that clear?"

Damn, this man was harsh. Scary, intense, and yeah, even sexy in that way dominant men had. This dude was alpha dog all the way.

"Clear as rain, Colonel. I want my life back. The only way to get that is through Victor Conti. If that means taking shit from a bunch of military top-dog assholes to get it, then I'm your girl." She smiled to soften the blow even while she cursed herself six ways to Sunday for taking the chance. She didn't need to piss this guy off. Not now. Not before she'd even set foot in Africa.

Mendez barked a laugh. It was so unexpected that she flinched before she could stop herself. She hoped he hadn't seen it. She glanced at Alex Bishop. He was grinning, though trying to hide it behind his hand. He lifted a brow at her, and she knew he'd seen her jump.

"You can take the shit or shovel the shit, I don't care which it is so long as you follow orders and don't cause trouble for my SEALs. But this operation is dangerous, Agent Wood, more dangerous than you or your handler perhaps realize. We'll do our best to make sure you come back, but there's no guarantee." He paused for a long moment, and she felt the blood rushing in her veins. "Now, if you'd like to stay home, I can arrange that. Ms. Spencer doesn't even need to know."

Miranda refused to let him see how annoyed she was at the suggestion. She smiled as warmly as she could manage. She wasn't giving up. Not now. Not ever. This man would know that by the end.

"No, thank you. I'm going."

"Then we've got no time to waste." He looked at his watch. "There's a mission briefing in half an hour."

He stood. This time she didn't move. "Colonel…" Her pulse quickened.

"Yes, Agent Wood?"

"Cody… will he be on this mission as well?"

"He will. He's a professional though. And he's been told your death was a ruse. He understands why it had to happen."

"I… uh, I'd like to talk to him. Before everything gets

crazy, I mean. Is that possible?"

Mendez glanced at Alex Bishop. Something must have passed between them because Alex said, "I'll get him, sir."

Once he was gone, Mendez gave her a hard look. It wasn't unfriendly, but it wasn't warm either. "It was a damned rotten thing to do, though I'm as much at fault as anyone because I went along with it."

"It wasn't my choice. I was following orders." She hoped he understood the significance of that statement. She'd followed orders. She *would* follow orders even when she didn't like the order. Because she wasn't stupid and she was well trained. As well trained as his people, even if he didn't think so. "If I had it to do over… Well, I'd still follow orders, but I'd fight harder for a different way."

He nodded. "Good to know. I understand you wanting to talk to him, but don't be surprised if he's unwilling to forgive you for it. McCormick's a good SEAL. He thought he was helping you. He's not going to be happy about being deceived, no matter the reason for it."

Miranda swallowed the knot in her throat. Why did she care so much? He was nothing to her. They were nothing to each other. They'd had sex. That was it. And yet the thought of Cody looking at her with contempt— Well, that managed to make her feel rotten.

"I understand, Colonel."

He studied her for a long moment. "I hope you do, Agent Wood. I sincerely hope you do."

Cody stopped outside the conference room door. Miranda was inside. Miranda, the woman he'd thought was dead for the past six weeks. The woman he'd thought he'd failed. She was fucking alive. She'd faked her own death. With the help of Samantha Spencer and the CIA, she'd faked it right there in the desert and left him to deal with the consequences.

Oh, he knew she'd been told to do it. That Samantha had the idea Miranda needed to be dead to smoke out the mole. But fucking hell, she'd never thought once about telling him what was going down?

Not fair, Cody. She was obeying orders.

Yeah, fuck. Orders. He knew all about tough orders. And yet he'd thought maybe there was something more between them. Some level of trust that meant they had each other's backs. He didn't know why he'd thought that, come to think of it. She'd never once given him any reason to believe he could trust her. She'd been vulnerable that night at the safe house. She'd told him about her childhood, about Mark Reed. And then she'd melted in his arms.

No reason to think there was trust between them.

A wall of anger built inside him, swelling outward, threatening his cool. He had half a hangover and he was cranky as hell. He didn't bother knocking. He simply twisted the knob and pushed the door in. A woman whirled toward him. She was standing near the far wall, her fingers clenching a cup of water. For a moment he couldn't believe it was her. She had red hair, not gold. Shoulder length, not the long locks she'd had before. Her eyes were green instead of whiskey-gold.

But the face was Miranda's. The line of her jaw, the slight tilt of her nose. The plump, pink mouth with the little bow in her top lip.

She blinked at him, her chest rising and falling a little faster than normal, or so he thought. Her lips were parted ever so slightly, as if she wasn't sure what to say now that they were face-to-face. She wore a white button-down and black slacks. She looked like a fucking government agent.

She is *a government agent.*

"Hi," she said softly, her voice quavering just a fraction. Those pink lips parted in a smile. He hardened his heart as he stared at her. Because, fuck, he wanted to take her in his arms and hold her tight. He wanted to bury his face in her hair and squeeze her to him.

The last time he'd seen her, she'd been bleeding out on an Arizona dirt road.

Except she hadn't been bleeding out at all. Fake blood. Capsules fired from a modified gun at close range. Remembering how empty and helpless he'd felt, and that it had all been a ruse, helped to keep his anger alive in that moment.

"I'm glad you aren't dead," he said coolly.

She swallowed visibly. "I'm glad too."

Her tongue darted out to lick her lips, and his groin tightened. Fucking hell, no way. It wasn't fair.

"I'm sorry, Cody. I did what I was told—but I hated it."

"You didn't hate it enough to tell me the truth."

"That's not fair. I was obeying orders. I couldn't tell you the truth."

He snorted as he stalked into the room. He kept his hands shoved into his pockets just in case he was tempted to reach for her. "I went out of my way to help you, Miranda. I was ready to fight for you."

Her brows drew low for a second. "Don't lie to me, Cody."

"Like you lied to me?"

She took a step forward, then halted abruptly. Her face twisted in anger and pain. "You were going to take me in! You'd been ordered to do it, and you would have done what you were told to do. Don't tell me you wouldn't. Don't you dare tell me you'd have disobeyed a direct order from that very scary colonel you call a boss."

It was his turn to swallow. "I wasn't going to abandon you. I told you I'd help clear your name, and I meant it."

She scoffed. "You'd have done what you were told, the same as I did. Don't try to tell me otherwise. You got a call that morning, just like I did. You didn't tell me what it was about. You didn't tell me you'd been ordered to turn me over to Sam at the Vegas airport."

He gritted his teeth. "I was working on it. There was still time."

She set the cup down and folded her arms beneath her breasts. Those lush breasts with the thick, gorgeous nipples he'd sucked until she'd squirmed and cried out beneath him.

Goddamn. Don't think about that.

Because thinking about it made the blood rush to his cock.

"You would have come up empty-handed, cowboy,

and you know it. There was no way out. For either of us."

He swore. And then he glared at her. "I watched you fucking get shot to death out there, Miranda. Even if I'd taken you in as ordered, you'd have been alive. I wouldn't have spent six weeks living with the memory of your death or the fact I couldn't save you. Do you have any idea how hard that was? How much I blamed myself for not preventing you from walking out in front of the truck like that?"

He thought for a second her eyes were glittering. Tears? But then she sucked in a breath and picked up her water again. She took a sip, her eyes downcast. When she finished, she fixed him with a green stare that was more than a little bit disconcerting. Miranda's eyes but not Miranda's eyes.

"I can't fix that, and I'm sorry. But we both know how this game is played. We know what we are, Cody. I did what I had to do the same as you would. The same as you *will*. We're warriors in a fight bigger than we are. We adapt and improvise, and we hopefully come out alive. I want Victor Conti, and I want to know who betrayed me. That's why I'm here. I hope we can work together and that this won't be a problem between us."

He could only gape at her. A problem between them? She'd fucking pretended to get *shot* in front of him, and now she wanted to just sail on as if it was simply something that had to be done?

He closed the distance between them because he was furious, because he couldn't quite stop himself. Because he wanted a reaction, goddammit. He wanted her to flinch, to blink, to do something. Anything. She took a step back as he loomed over her. Her pulse throbbed in her neck.

That satisfied him.

It also made him angry with himself. What kind of man was he that he used his size and strength to intimidate a woman?

He rocked back on his heels and gave her space. He didn't miss that her gaze darted to his chest—and lower. For a fraction of a second, she glanced at his groin. But then she met his eyes evenly, her green ones somber and resigned.

"I hate those fucking contacts," he growled because he couldn't say any of the other things he wanted to say. "They aren't you."

Her breath hitched. "I think that's the point."

"The hair is hot though." Now shit, where had that come from?

She dropped her gaze. "Thanks. I hated cutting it—but it's just hair."

"Where did they send you?" he asked, trying to cut through the mire of feelings rolling through him.

"Luxembourg. I spent time tapping into Victor's banking files. He's been transferring a lot of money to Jorwani."

Cody frowned. "I'd have thought it was the other way around. Okonjo had to get his guns from somewhere."

If he stared hard enough, he could almost see the whiskey color of her eyes beneath the green. Though he was probably only fooling himself. She wouldn't look at him for long though. A few seconds and then her gaze would dart away again.

"Yes, we all thought that. But the money is definitely transferring in. He's buying something."

"Any thoughts on your mole?"

Her gaze whipped to his again. Her lips parted. And then she shook her head. "He or she is very careful. Not a peep in weeks."

"Until Conti fled the country."

"Right."

There was a knock at the door. Cody went over and jerked it open. Money stood there with a sober look on his face.

"Been sent to fetch you both. We've got our orders. Bugging out in six hours."

CHAPTER NINETEEN

MIRANDA FELT AS if she had whiplash. First she'd been fetched from the nondescript agency apartment she'd been staying in, driven to HOT HQ, and dropped at the gate. She'd endured security checks, fingerprinting, and eye scans. She'd been tag-teamed by a pair of colonels the likes of which were enough to make grown men cry.

And then she'd been thrown into a room—at her request, it was true—with a very tall, very hot, very angry SEAL. Just when she'd thought they might be making progress, another tall, hot, and not angry SEAL had come along and hauled them to a briefing room where she had to endure many eyes upon her as she walked in.

"We have the CIA with us today," Mendez said. "This is Agent Jane Wood, and she'll be accompanying us to Jorwani."

There was a soft grumbling in the room, but Miranda kept her head up and refused to acknowledge it. She figured many—if not all of them—knew who she really was, but when you were undercover, you went by that identity all the time so there were no mistakes when it mattered most.

Introductions were quickly made. There were nine SEALs total—and nine other men who were introduced as Alpha Squad. There were also two women, which both surprised and fascinated her. So far as she knew, women weren't yet allowed in the Special Ops. Oh, she'd seen the news of the female Rangers, like everyone had, and she'd cheered them on. But there were, what, three of them?

Rangers were badass as hell—but they weren't the ultrasecret Hostile Operations Team. She'd have bet a kidney that she'd find no women here.

But here they were. A tawny blonde named Lucky with fine silver scars on both her arms, and a stunning redhead named Victoria. Miranda would need time to sort out all the men, but she wouldn't forget the women's names. Lucky smiled at her, but Victoria only arched a sculpted eyebrow. Miranda arched one back as if to say she didn't give a fuck.

She didn't much care what anyone thought of her, quite honestly—except Cody, dammit. She cared what he thought, and that annoyed her as much as it perplexed her.

Cody went over and flung himself into a seat like a moody teenager. Miranda let her gaze slide over the group and then went and took one of the only empty seats left.

Miranda settled in and waited for Colonel Mendez and Lieutenant Colonel Bishop to begin the briefing. Mendez looked over at someone and the lights went down. A slide show flickered to life on the giant screen against one wall.

There was a picture of Zain Okonjo, a brutal, conscienceless warlord who'd killed as many people as he'd liberated when he overthrew the government of Jorwani. He was laughing and pointing at the cheering crowd arrayed before him. It was an official video, of course, so it would not show him in a bad light.

"Zain Okonjo overthrew the government of Jorwani six months ago. Since then, his army has killed an estimated one hundred thousand Jorwani citizens using a combination of chemical weapons and automatic rifles. They've enslaved children, sold girls into sexual servitude, and threatened the region with instability. Unfortunately, Okonjo is not our target."

There was a collective grumble in the room.

"The United Nations has enacted economic sanctions against the Okonjo government. The US is not sending in troops at this time." Mendez paused while everyone considered that statement. "We have no forward bases in Jorwani. No support systems. There's an unofficial group operating in the area. They'll be our contact throughout the mission."

"Ian Black, sir?" one of the men said.

Miranda listened with interest. She knew who Ian Black was. She'd heard the name before, from Mark and from Badger. Ian Black was former CIA, disavowed, a rogue of the worst sort. But apparently not a traitor—or not a dumb one, because he'd never been arrested.

"Yes, Black's group is there and they have intel we'll need on the ground. When you cross the border into Jorwani, you'll be on your own. Okonjo's government is still allowing aid organizations in, so that will be your cover. Our target—"

Here a picture of Victor Conti flashed onto the screen.

"—is Victor Conti, an Italian-American businessman with known ties to illegal weapons dealing, drugs, and human trafficking for purposes of sexual slavery. He is currently a guest of Mr. Okonjo, staying in his presidential palace." Mendez turned back to the screen as a vast compound appeared. "We're working on a schematic of the building now, as well as a report on Okonjo's security. In five days' time, Okonjo is scheduled to attend a summit in Kenya. The security for that trip is tight, and Okonjo's schedule has been set for weeks. Victor Conti won't be with him, which means the palace will be as vulnerable as it'll ever get. That's our opportunity."

"How can we be sure, sir, that Conti won't go with him?" This question came from a blond man who conjured up mental images from the movie *Thor*.

Mendez's expression was sober. "As of 0800 this morning, Conti is wanted by Kenyan authorities for human trafficking and weapons smuggling within their borders. He won't set foot into Kenya." He turned back to the screen. "You'll have to enter Jorwani in groups of four and five. Due to the nature of Jorwani cultural beliefs, the women will need to be married when they enter the country."

Miranda glanced at Victoria since she was closest. A man sitting beside her laid his hand on her leg and squeezed. Well, okay then, not a problem for her. Probably not a problem for Lucky either. They knew these guys. She did not.

She purposely didn't look at Cody, though she couldn't imagine pretending to be a couple with anyone but him. Still, it was probably better if she was paired with someone else. Someone who didn't make her pulse—and other parts of her—throb.

"Who's pretending to be married to the CIA agent, sir?"

It was Cody's voice, and Miranda's belly tightened on cue.

Mendez raised a brow. "Whoever volunteers to do the job. Is that gonna be you, McCormick?"

His silence was telling.

"I'll do it, sir," a voice said. Miranda turned to see the SEAL who'd come to get her and Cody earlier. He was too pretty for words, but he didn't make her pulse quicken the way Cody did.

"Good luck," Cody muttered, and disappointment crashed through her.

"Then it's settled. Cash is the lucky groom. Any other questions?" Mendez asked. No one said a word.

He spoke for several more minutes, clicking through slides as he did so, but all Miranda could think about was the fact she was about to enter a dangerous country with a man at her side—and not the man she preferred.

Dammit, when had her life gotten so complicated? Before she'd jabbed her gun into Cody's side in the Venetian, she'd known exactly what she was doing and exactly what to expect. She'd wanted to get to the truth behind Mark's death and take down Victor Conti. All she'd managed to do was get herself "killed" and watch Conti flee to Africa. She wasn't any closer to what she wanted at all.

And now she was wound tight and worrying over the fact that a man she'd slept with, a man who'd gotten through her defenses and made her feel something other than anger and pain, didn't want to pretend to be her husband on a mission. Really?

It was a low point in her life and career, that's for sure.

"That's everything," Mendez said, snapping her attention back to him. He looked at his watch. "It's five hours to go time. You know what to do. Dismissed."

Cody folded himself into the van and put on his headphones. He didn't want to talk to anyone right now. He didn't know which van Miranda was in as they lurched forward, and he didn't care. They were on their way to Joint Base Andrews where they would board a military transport headed for Germany. They had too much gear and too many people to get a commercial flight. But it was also faster because they could fly straight to Ramstein where they'd pick up another transport to the American base in Djibouti.

It was also more private, which he preferred. They were taking a C-5 Galaxy, which meant jump seats anchored into the cargo bay. There were no windows. No flight attendants. No beverage cart or screaming kids. There were boxed meals and drinks, and it was pretty much self-service.

There were also no assigned seats. That meant he could take a seat as far away from Miranda as possible. He didn't want anything to do with her. Hell, if he thought about it hard enough, he could pretend that woman wasn't Miranda Lockwood at all. Jane Wood had green eyes and shoulder-length red hair. Miranda had whiskey eyes and gold hair. Not the same woman.

When they arrived at the flight line on Andrews, everyone piled from the vans and dragged out their duffels and the rest of the gear. The jet was already warming the engines as Miranda emerged from a van with Money, who'd wasted no time getting cozy with her. She smiled at him, her arms folded beneath her breasts.

Cody saw red. Then she tilted her head back and laughed at something Money said—and a hot, possessive feeling blossomed in Cody's soul. A feeling that said *mine*.

What the fuck?

He deliberately turned away and hefted an equipment bag, carrying it over to the pile waiting to be stowed on the plane. When he turned back, Money had leaned in to say something to Miranda. She laughed again, her head back, her throat exposed to the waning sunlight.

Dammit, he'd kissed that throat. Heard words issue from it that tightened his balls and made him lose whatever control he'd had. Damn, but fucking her had been sweet. So sweet.

He wanted to do it again. And again.

No. No way in hell. She was bad news. She'd gotten to him with her talk of growing up with an alcoholic mother, leaving home, and leaving everyone behind. Stripping to stay alive and then being saved by a CIA agent who became her mentor and friend.

Don't forget he was her lover too.

A lover she was still so wound up about that she'd risked her life to find the person who'd had him killed. Cody figured that if Mark Reed had still been alive, Miranda wouldn't have kept any secrets from *him.* No, she'd have told him she was about to fake her death so she could disappear.

Money did that thing where he pretended to tuck a stray lock of hair behind a woman's ear. Before Cody knew what he was doing, he strode over to where Miranda smiled up at his teammate. She must have sensed him coming because she glanced in his direction—and her smile faded.

"This is a serious mission, for fuck's sake," he growled when he reached the two of them. "Not a pickup bar."

Money gave him a look that said *Oh yeah* and *What you gonna do about it, motherfucker?*

"I think you've overstepped your authority to tell me what to do—which is precisely none, by the way," Miranda said, sniffing in his general direction.

"It is if you're going to act like a fucking teenager on a date," Cody grated. "This is serious shit."

"Hey, that's my wife you're talking to," Money said, brows drawing down like he was spoiling for a fight.

Cody shook his head. Money wasn't seriously pissed, and they both knew it. "Not yet, she's not. Lay off until we get to Jorwani. You can get cuddly there."

Miranda crossed her arms and glared at him. Her eyes sparked fire.

Money didn't seem to notice. "If you don't like the way I'm doing it, *you* shack up with her for the mission."

Cody stared hard at Miranda. She stared right back, never backing down for a second. And Jesus, his groin started to tighten, the familiar tingle at the base of his spine indicating where the blood was starting to go. A whirlwind of emotions gathered strength in his gut. If he let them out, if he faced them— No, not going there. He was pissed. Nothing more.

And he didn't care what she did. Or who she did it with.

"Nope. She's yours, man. Happy anniversary and all that shit."

He turned and strode away, back to the equipment they were starting to load on the massive plane. The nose assembly was up for cargo loading, and he grabbed two huge bags and walked up the ramp. He stowed them with the others and then went to find a seat, nodding at the loadmaster as he passed. There were several rows, five across, and seats also lined the walls. The center seats could be anchored in or taken out, depending on how many troops they were moving, and they faced rear, which was weird the first few times you did it. The load today was mostly cargo, with HOT and maybe a few Space-A fliers. There was another passenger compartment at the rear of the plane, but that one was much noisier than up here—colder too. If there were seats forward, then Cody always took them.

His teammates piled in and found seats. The engines spooled up a little bit louder now, and Cody popped his headphones on again. He looked up as Money and Miranda walked by and sat in the row in front of him. He closed his eyes and tried to sleep, but her scent stole to him, wrapped around his senses. She smelled fresh and clean, like a flowery shampoo. It wasn't overpowering, but it was too close. He started to get up and move but stubbornly decided to stay right where he was. He wasn't letting her chase him away.

Cody opened his eyes as someone flopped down beside him. It was Remy Marchand.

"Hey, man, you look pissed off."

"Just tired."

"No, pissed. And still a little bit hungover, yeah?"

Cody tried not to think about the slight throb in his temples. "Nah, not too bad."

"You realize Money's just trying to get your goat, dude." He glanced around the room as if seeing who was close enough to listen and then back to Cody. "He doesn't know it for sure—only Viking and I do—but I'm pretty sure he suspects she's the girl you were helping in the desert based on your reactions to her. And we all know how fucked up everything got out there. You haven't been the same since it happened. Money's trying to shake you loose."

Cody wanted to growl. "What do you expect? A woman I promised to help got killed and I couldn't stop it. Except she didn't get killed. Here she fucking is—and she's laughing at Money's jokes like he's goddamn Robin Williams reincarnated."

Cage's mouth twisted into a grin. "Well, he can be pretty funny sometimes—but today he's yanking your chain. Because *you* want to be the one sitting up there with her. You just don't want to admit it."

A wave of anger swelled in his belly. Why did everyone think he gave two shits about Miranda Lockwood or Jane Wood or whoever the fuck she was pretending to be today? He was done caring. He knew what happened when he did, and it hadn't been pretty.

"No, I really fucking don't."

Cage shrugged. The loadmaster stopped and instructed him to put on his seatbelt. "Yeah, sorry, got it," Cage said, clipping it in place. He whipped out his phone and started punching buttons. "Did I show you the picture of Elvis serenading me and Christina at the wedding?"

Cody sank deeper into his seat like a turtle trying to pull his head in. It was going to be a long-ass flight. "Yeah, I believe you did. Not to mention I was actually there for the wedding."

"Then look at this one of the honeymoon."

Cody frowned. "You sure about that, dude?"

Cage rolled his eyes. "Not the actual honeymoon, you moron. The hotel. The food."

The engines began to whine, and the plane started its lumbering progress down the taxiway. Only a million more hours of being confined in this tin can and smelling Miranda's shampoo. Yay.

CHAPTER TWENTY

BY THE TIME they reached Djibouti, Miranda was more than ready for a hot shower and some decent sleep. She'd tried to nap on the trip, and there had been plenty of seats to stretch out and do so, but it hadn't been easy with the whine of the engines and the utter lack of heat. Flying in a military plane wasn't like flying commercial. The temperature control was practically nonexistent, though they claimed to have heat. The blanket she'd been given hadn't been enough to warm her up, and she'd spent much of each flight shivering.

And now she was hot. Djibouti wasn't exactly an alpine nation. With average daily temperatures between ninety and 106, this place was smoking. The terrain was flat, dusty and dirty and rocky, and the base was a combination of military tan, dirty white, and stacks of what looked like shipping containers but were really barracks or Containerized Housing Units. The base shared a runway with the Djibouti airport, so at least the trip wasn't far from landing to lodging.

They weren't taken to the CHUs though. They were taken to a special compound much like the HOT headquarters back in DC where they had to pass through layers of security. Though not as sophisticated a facility, it was still heavily guarded. Lucky sidled up beside her as they walked down a hallway and told her this was a HOT facility. Then she smiled reassuringly and Miranda smiled in return.

She wasn't scared, but she wouldn't turn down a gesture of friendliness from one of the women on this mission. She wondered about the other woman's scars, but she knew better than to ask.

"Have you been here before?"

"Once or twice."

"I didn't realize we had women in Special Ops."

Lucky shrugged. "Not enough of us, that's for sure." She stopped at a door and opened it. "This is us in here."

Miranda stepped into the small room. There were four bunks inside, a light, and a table. To say it didn't even compare to the worst budget hotel in America was probably an understatement.

Lucky slung her bag to the floor and sat down on one of the mattresses. "Jesus, I'm so tired I could sleep in my clothes. Hell, I just might."

Miranda set her bag down. "Is it just us in here?"

Lucky opened an eye. "Victoria will be here as soon as she finishes copping a feel of her husband."

Miranda blinked. "Husband? She's on a mission with her husband?"

She thought of the big dude sitting next to Victoria in the briefing and the way he'd squeezed her leg.

Lucky laughed. “We both are. Victoria’s married to Nick Brandon, Alpha Squad’s sniper. Kev MacDonald is my husband. Also Alpha Squad,” she added. “Kev’s the second-in-command.”

“And you and Victoria are Alpha Squad too?”

“We’re freelancers, so to speak. We go when needed.”

“Isn’t that a little difficult? Working with your spouse, I mean?”

“Sometimes. Mostly we just do our jobs.”

The door opened and Victoria walked in, looking as cool as a cucumber even in this heat. Miranda wondered how she did it. Victoria threw her duffel on the floor and sat on the only other lower bunk.

“I’ve just been telling Jane about our husbands,” Lucky said. “I think she’s a little stunned.”

Victoria snorted. “I sometimes think they’re still a bit stunned too. Nick actually spent about an hour on the flight asking me if I didn’t want to hang out here while they went to Jorwani. I finally shut him down, but not before I threatened to cut him off for a month—or six.”

Lucky laughed. “Oh yes, that would do it for Kev as well. He knows better than to even try these days.”

Victoria turned and fixed her with a stare. “What about you, Jane? Got a man in your life?”

Miranda wasn’t sure if the question was genuine or if everyone knew about her and Cody and this was simply Victoria’s way of digging at her. “Not at the moment.”

“Looked like you were getting cozy with Cash. He’s a nice guy, but don’t let him fool you—he’s a horndog. Probably stuck that thing in half the waitresses back home. I’d think twice before I let him stick it in me.”

"I really wasn't planning on it," Miranda said. "He's nice enough, but…"

"He's no Cody McCormick," Lucky finished.

Miranda let herself look confused. "I'm sorry?"

Lucky glanced at Victoria, who smirked. "We couldn't help but notice the tension back at HQ and on the plane. Cody doesn't appear to like you, which is surprising since he usually likes everyone. And then there was the private meeting you had with him before the briefing." Her smile widened. "News travels in our circles."

"Clearly." But how much news?

"Now I don't know for sure," Lucky went on, "but I'm guessing you and the CIA agent Cody was with in the desert a few weeks ago are one and the same. He didn't tell us the death was a fake, by the way."

Miranda felt like a balloon someone had pierced with a straight pin. Did she keep up the pretense or admit what these two women already knew? On the one hand, she was conditioned to keep everything close to the vest. Never let anyone see your hand.

But at the same time, fuck it, what did it matter? They were all on the same side, she had no doubts about that at all, and she was tired of acting like nothing ever got under her skin when Cody seemed to be the exception.

"He didn't know," she admitted.

Lucky sat up abruptly.

Victoria's brows drew down. "He didn't know? You mean he thought you were dead for real?"

Miranda sank onto the lone chair in the room. It was metal and not all that comfortable. "Yes. That's why I met with him. To apologize."

Victoria whistled. "Lordy, lordy. No wonder he

seemed so pissed off. Girl, that man is HOT through and through—they are the best of the best—and he's not going to take it well that you kept the truth from him. These guys are tough and loyal to a fault. But you jerk one around—Jesus, it doesn't go down well. And yes, I speak from experience."

Lucky raised a hand. "Me too. Though nothing so terrible as faking my own death. But I did jerk Kev around a bit, that's for sure."

Miranda's throat was tight. And she felt strangely relieved too. She had five sisters, but she never talked to them anymore—except for the next oldest to her, whom she talked to about once a year. She'd always felt like a substitute mother rather than a sister, especially to the younger girls, and she'd fled the first chance she got. To actually have women to talk to like they were friends?

It was nice. Oh, she knew they weren't really friends and this wasn't the beginning of a lifetime of girl chats. But it worked for now.

"I don't know how to fix it," she confessed, giving in for once to the little voice that urged her to share.

"Do you want to? Or do you just want him to forgive you so you feel better?" Victoria was looking at her intently. "Because there is a difference. You want to fix it for him because you care that you hurt him, or you want to bury it under the rug and have his forgiveness so you don't have to feel bad anymore."

"I care that I hurt him. If he hadn't helped me in Vegas, I'd be dead for real. I owe him better."

Lucky scratched her cheek. "Well then. Guess we're going to have to think of something, aren't we?"

Victoria nodded. "Absolutely. And we're going to

start by getting him to take Cash's place on this mission. Cody has to be the one spending time with you, not Cash."

Miranda shook her head. "Cash asked him straight up if he wanted the job back on Andrews. He said no."

Lucky waved her hand dismissively. "Of course he did. But that is about to end, isn't it, Vee?"

"Hell yes it is. We've got this."

Miranda let her gaze slide between them. She wasn't accustomed to this. At all. "I appreciate that you want to help—but why do y'all even care? You don't know me. Maybe I'm a royal bitch and Cody's better off hating me."

"Cody's one of the easiest-going people I know," Victoria said. "But he hasn't been the same the past few weeks. So either he gets you out of his system and moves on, or he doesn't and y'all work out your shit. Avoidance solves nothing. Trust me, I know *that* from personal experience too."

"Yep, have to second that," Lucky said. "Life is easier when you confront your problems head-on. If I'd gotten away with avoiding my issues, I'd still be in Hawaii and I wouldn't have married Kev. Believe me when I say I far prefer the life I have now."

"I'm not— I don't feel that way about him," Miranda said. "This isn't about getting together or getting married. Just so you know." But even as she said it, her belly tightened.

Victoria arched one of those expressive eyebrows of hers. "Of course not, honey," she said. "That's never what it's about. It's just how it ends up."

“Man, that woman is hot, hot, hot,” Money said as they stood in the shower together. It was the next morning after they’d arrived and the SEALs were getting ready for the day. They’d do some last minute massaging of the plan based on intel, and then they’d board commercial flights into Jorwani, separating into smaller groups so that they didn’t all enter at the same time. Once there, they were to head to the aid organization’s headquarters and regroup.

“That ass, those tits, those lips… Christ, what I wouldn’t give to get up in that.”

Cody grunted and turned his back as Money extolled Miranda’s virtues. What he really wanted to do was wrap his hands around Money’s neck and squeeze.

Alex “Camel” Kamarov chimed in. “Dude, smart of you to volunteer to hang with her. Maybe when you’re pretending to be married, you can actually do the deed, you know?”

Cody whirled. “You two need to shut the fuck up. There’s no time for that shit. We go in, we finish our plan so it’s airtight, we get Conti, and get out.”

“Man, he can bang her in the next night or two. We’ve got three nights until Okonjo leaves, so why not?” Camel said. “He can bang her all three nights.”

“Nobody’s banging anybody,” Cody said. “Jesus Christ, are you two on a mission or playing a fucking video game? You can’t pause this shit to get your freak on and then unpause and go back to the action.”

"I think that's up to me and the lady," Money said, soaping his chest. "Why do you care, anyway?"

"I don't."

Cody turned the taps to let colder water stream over him. He was getting pissed and needed to cool his temper. Money merely grinned, the bastard. Cody turned his back and rinsed off, then shut off the taps and grabbed his towel. He dried vigorously, scrubbing his head and body, then yanked on his clothes—civvies since they were flying into Jorwani later this afternoon—and grabbed his bag before heading back down the hallway to the bunk room he shared with Money, Camel, and Adam "Blade" Garrison.

He left everything and headed to the mess hall where he grabbed a tray and then went down the line, grabbing eggs, bacon, toast, and coffee. Then he went over and plunked the whole thing down on a table. He was doing a good job of eating and not thinking about the things Money had said when Miranda sailed into the room, looking cool and fresh in a summery dress that went down to her ankles and was held up by a tube of fabric clinging to her ample breasts. Oh Lord have mercy.

Victoria and Lucky were with her. Also wearing dresses. Also looking cool and fresh.

"Dude, you do know your eyes are bugging out of your head, right?"

Cody swiveled to find Viking sitting down beside him. Cage took the seat across from them. Cody dropped his fork onto the plate.

"I'm pissed off, all right? Is that what you assholes want to hear? She fucking lied to me, and I've spent six whole weeks wondering what the fuck I could have done differently. How I could have saved her. Turns out she didn't need saving, that she cooked up this whole god-damned thing with Samantha Spencer and her people. It was a ruse, and I was the dupe."

Viking's eyebrows climbed his forehead during Cody's speech. "Totally get that, Cowboy. You're pissed, and you have every right. But you don't look at that woman like you're pissed."

Cody blinked. "Sure feels like I'm pissed."

Cage laughed, then leaned in and lowered his voice. "I say this with love, man, but the truth is you want to get into those panties pretty badly."

"So does Money," he snapped. "Doesn't mean it's gonna happen."

Cage dug his fork into his eggs. Then he looked at Cody. "So you gonna let him have the chance, huh? All cozied up with her for three days before we infiltrate the compound. Sounds reasonable."

His chest tightened almost unbearably. Let Money spend three days with Miranda in close quarters? After everything he'd said in the shower? No fucking way.

"No."

"No?" Viking asked, looking amused as he stabbed some fried potatoes.

Cody blew out a breath and picked up his fork again. Goddammit. "No, I'm not letting Money have a chance. I'll take the assignment. I'll be her partner for the trip."

CHAPTER TWENTY-ONE

MIRANDA WENT OUTSIDE at the appointed time to meet Cash. They were going to the airport and boarding a flight to Jorwani along with Lucky and her husband, Kevin MacDonald. Lucky'd said she'd have Miranda's new documents. She was still Jane instead of Miranda, but now she would be Jane McQuaid, wife of Cash McQuaid. The documents were forged with state of-the-art equipment in record time, but she'd have expected nothing different from a black-ops group.

She opened the door and went out to the parking lot with her bag. She had clothes, but no weapons. None of them did. They'd get weapons once in-country from their contact there. Miranda hated how out of the loop she felt with this group, but she was here to make sure the CIA got their piece of Conti. And she would. It was the only way she'd ever get her life back.

Not that she'd had much of a life, she reflected. She'd lived for work, immersed herself in it. She had no identity outside of the CIA anymore. Not for the first time over the past few weeks, she thought of her sisters back in Alabama. She'd walked away eight years ago, and she hadn't looked back.

But maybe she'd been too eager, too certain of what she wanted when she was still too young to really know. Maybe she needed to call them more than once a year.

Miranda stopped under an awning and dropped her small suitcase at her feet. She turned to look at the building. The door opened and a familiar form swaggered out, tall and Hollywood handsome, making her heart trip over itself as it tried to beat normally.

Dammit, why did she let the sight of Cody get to her like this? Whatever they'd had in the desert had been an anomaly. Yeah, she knew what it was like to lie beneath him and feel the power of his body moving inside hers. And holy hell but that thought made her breath shorten.

The heat, the skin, the pleasure. What she wouldn't give to experience that again. Just once. Was that too much to ask?

He was carrying a duffel, striding toward her with purpose. She watched him approach, mentally undressing him as he did. His blue eyes lasered in on her, his scowl hard and cold. And then he was there, dropping his bag and looking at her with poorly disguised annoyance.

He wore a white button-down that clung to the muscles of his torso and a pair of khakis that reminded her just how gorgeous and firm that ass was. The door opened again and Lucky and Kev emerged, moving toward them.

Miranda's gaze flickered to them and then back to Cody. Were there five of them going this round instead of four?

"If you're looking for Money, he's not coming."

Miranda blinked. "I beg your pardon?"

Cody's expression was militant. As if he were being forced to do something he definitely did not want to do. "Money. Cash. He's not coming. You're Jane McCormick now."

"What happened? Is he okay?"

Cody shoved a hand through his dark hair, his muscles flexing as he did so, and a bolt of fire raced through her limbs. "He's fine. Turns out I'm the better choice for this job."

"If that's the case, why are you so grumpy about it?"

He speared her with that blue gaze. "Who said I'm grumpy?"

Miranda snorted. "Really? You don't think you're coming off as pissed?"

"I'm not pissed. I'm annoyed."

"And that's different how?" she asked.

But he didn't answer because Lucky and Kev reached them then. Lucky looked smug. "Here are your papers, Mrs. McCormick."

Miranda wanted to ask how in the hell they'd worked so fast to get Cody to take this job, but she could hardly do it with him standing there. A current of happiness swirled through her. Cody was here. With her. Pissed, sure. But he was here and that meant she had a chance to make this right.

And that was all she wanted. Just to make it right. It had nothing to do with those broad shoulders, those sculpted lips, or the hands that had taken her to heights she hadn't experienced with any other man. Nothing whatsoever to do with that chiseled body or the huge cock that he knew how to use to bring the most pleasure to any woman lucky enough to get naked with him.

Miranda tucked the new fake passport into her purse as a van turned the corner and rolled toward them. Kev grabbed his and Lucky's bags and headed for the rear of the van as it came to a stop.

Miranda reached for her bag, but Cody was there first. He snatched hers up along with his and then went and put them in the back. Miranda climbed into the last row and set her purse on her lap. She was wearing a maxi dress when she'd rather be wearing pants, but she was supposed to look the part of a wife going to Jorwani to help provide aid to the population. She'd change into pants after today, but the first impression she wanted to give to the Jorwani authorities was of femininity and helplessness, bless their little misogynistic souls. She'd put on a cotton shirt over the dress and tied it at her waist in order to cover her shoulders, but the first chance she got she was taking it off. It was hot and sweat trickled between her breasts just from that brief time outside.

Cody stopped in the doorway and looked at her. Then he climbed in and sank down beside her, leaving the only other row for Lucky and Kev. His leg brushed against hers and a shudder went through her. She clutched her purse and turned her head to gaze out the window. The terrain was brown and dusty, and a haze hung over everything. It was the humidity in the air from the Gulf of Aden. Jorwani would be no better.

Kev and Lucky climbed into the van and the door slid shut. Lucky turned and smiled.

"Are we having fun yet?" she asked cheerfully.

Cody grunted and folded his arms over his chest. Miranda returned Lucky's smile. "Loads."

"That's what I thought. Let's get this over with and get back home in time for the weekend."

Kev put his arm around her and tugged her in close. She laid her head on his shoulder, and Miranda sighed. They were so comfortable together. So right. Lucky had intimated she'd jerked her husband around at one point—presumably before they were married—but looking at them now, Miranda couldn't imagine it. They seemed perfectly matched.

She had no idea what that was like. She'd never felt that way with anyone. Not even Mark. That had been a bit of hero worship and not feeling like she belonged anywhere else. It was easy to see in retrospect, but of course she hadn't known it at the time.

And maybe that was the problem. Maybe you couldn't ever know that what you felt was real, or that the person you felt it for also felt the same for you. It had to be a happy accident when two people like Kev and Lucky seemed to have it figured out.

Before long, they reached the airport. Once they were through security, they didn't have too long to wait before boarding the flight to Jorwani. A few of the other guys were at the gate waiting to board as well, but they didn't acknowledge each other. Not that anyone was watching or would even know to watch, but once in character it was best to stay. Standard operating procedure in her world.

She found her seat and started to lift her case over her head, but Cody snapped it up and stowed it for her. Then he shoved his in with it while she took her seat. He sat beside her and buckled his seat belt. He had headphones in, and he leaned his head back and closed his eyes.

"I think if this is going to work the way it's supposed to, we have to talk to each other *sometime,* you stubborn ass of a man."

He cracked open an eye. Of course he'd heard her. He reached up and pulled the headphones out, dropped them into his lap. "So what do you want to talk about, sugar dumpling?"

Sugar dumpling?

"I don't care. I just think we need to look like we like each other, even if it isn't true."

His eyes sparked. "It isn't. Just so you know."

That stung even though she should have expected it. "I don't like you much either. You're arrogant, bossy, and cranky as hell. And that was back in Vegas. Here? Jesus, if you hate me so much, why the hell did you take Cash's place?"

"Liked him, did you?"

"Yes. He was nice. And funny. He didn't glare at me like he wanted to choke me all the time."

"Nope. He just wanted to fuck you."

Her ears burned. Why? She wasn't a fainting virgin. But the thought of being intimate with any man now that she'd been intimate with this one seemed shocking and wrong somehow.

"Did you want to fuck him?" he asked, his expression hard.

"Would you care if I did?"

"Nope."

"Then why are you asking, asshole?"

"Just wondering if maybe that's your modus operandi. Get a guy to help you out while you play all vulnerable and sweet, fuck his brains out, and then hit him over the head with a two-by-four."

"A metaphorical two-by-four, of course."

"Of course."

The engines had revved up. Hearing anything besides the person sitting beside you was difficult, so she didn't worry about what she said next. "Yeah, that's what I do. It's so much fun putting all my trust in someone like Sam and hoping she doesn't plan to shoot me for real."

For the first time since she'd seen him again, his eyes softened. But only for a second. "If you'd shared what was happening with me, I'd have made sure it went down the way it was supposed to. I wouldn't have let her hurt you. She would have had to go through me to do it—and that wasn't going to happen."

Her pulse kicked up and her belly tightened. The thought of him protecting her from harm was utterly panty melting, even if she didn't need protecting. She could see the fierceness in his gaze, hear it in his voice. The conviction that he was stronger than everyone who might want to hurt her. The complete confidence in his skills as a warrior.

Yeah, panty melting.

"You aren't invincible, Cody," she said. "And I do know how to take care of myself. I've had as much training as you in self-defense."

He snorted. "I doubt that, baby doll. But yeah, you're a badass. I know you are, but I also know that badasses can't always do it all alone. Sometimes we need help."

She cocked an eyebrow. "Even you?"

"Yeah, even me. You met those other guys back in DC, right? The ones we arrived with yesterday"—he pointed across the aisle at Kev and Lucky, who were busy staring into each other's eyes—"those two over there. Those are teammates. I don't do this alone, honey."

Her eyes felt gritty for a second. "I did what I was told. Do I wish I'd done it differently? Yes. If I had it to do all over again, I'd tell you the minute I got off the phone with Sam. But I didn't tell you—and I can't go back in time."

He didn't say anything for a long moment. "Did you want to fuck him?"

After everything she'd just said, his words hit like a blow. She wanted to lash out at him, but she had nothing to lash out with. Nothing but the truth.

"No, Cody, I didn't. *I don't.* He was nice to me when you weren't. He didn't make me feel like a jerk the whole time he was with me. He didn't make me feel like I had to grovel at his feet."

"What you did to me—" He shook his head, his jaw hard where he clenched his teeth together. His voice was low and harsh. "I've seen a lot of death. Caused a few too. But I always knew what it was for, why it happened. With you—fuck, it wasn't right. I was numb—and yeah, I dreamed about you after that. Dreamed about touching you, kissing you, being inside you. Then I'd wake up and remember. And I'd want to fucking scream my head off."

Her throat ached with unshed tears. That surprised the hell out of her. She wasn't soft, and yet he made her feel soft in all the right places. "We hardly knew each other."

"It doesn't matter," he snapped. "We knew enough."

Miranda dropped her gaze. There was nothing she could say, nothing that would fix this. He was never going to forgive her. She had to live with that, with the knowledge she'd made it happen.

"You're right. I know you're right. These past few months..." She swallowed. "It's not an excuse, but I've been so used to working alone. Not knowing who to trust. I should have taken the chance, but I didn't. I'll regret it forever."

He gripped her chin, not hard, but firmly enough to pull her gaze to his. His touch was shocking. Comforting.

Arousing, damn him.

"I'm working with you because I didn't want Cash's hands on you. Not when I know how sweet you taste, how beautiful your passion is. I didn't want him to know what you sound like when you come or how pretty those nipples of yours are."

Her breath stopped. Just stopped. Her body responded to his voice, his words. Her nipples tightened and her pussy ached with arousal. Desire was a wave crashing over her, tugging her beneath the surface, stealing her breath and her ability to think about anything but the man sitting so close.

"What does that mean, Cody?"

His grip softened, his fingers sliding over her cheek, into her hair. He tugged a lock forward, rubbed it between his fingers. "This isn't you."

Her pulse raced. "No. But it's not permanent. And I'm still me inside." She put her fingers on his wrist. His pulse was strong too, and she knew he wasn't unaffected. "Why are you telling me this? What does it mean?"

His blue gaze met hers. The desire she saw there made her thighs tighten on the seat as if doing so could prevent the reaction between her legs.

"It means that even though I'm pissed at you, I'm glad you're alive. I'm glad they didn't succeed in putting out your fire."

"I'm glad too."

"I won't lie to you. I want to taste you again. I'm here because I couldn't stand the thought of Cash getting the opportunity to do to you all the things I still want to do."

"What do you want to do?" she asked.

His gaze dropped to her chest for a second, and her nipples hardened even more. The shirt was hiding her reaction, but he seemed to know it anyway.

"What do you want me to do?"

She hesitated. What if he was baiting her with the intent of shutting her down? Then again, so what if he did? It wouldn't be any worse than having him pissed at her these past couple of days. Besides, she didn't back down from a challenge.

"It's what I want to do to you," she said. "I didn't taste you the last time. I want to."

His nostrils flared. And then he leaned in and put his lips to her ear. A shiver rolled down her spine and into her limbs. "You want to suck my cock, Miranda?"

Her head swam. "Yes."

"Why me?" he asked, his breath tickling her ear. Sending more shivers over her. "Why not Cash?"

"Because… because it has to be you. Because he doesn't make my heart pound. Because even when you touch me like this, so lightly and simply, I want you so much it hurts. I don't know why I do, but I do."

He leaned back in his seat, breaking the contact. His eyes were hooded. But he shifted in his seat as if he were fighting a hard-on. "We hardly know each other," he said, echoing her words from earlier back to her. Mocking her.

Determination flooded her. "We know enough, Cody." She felt him pulling away even though he didn't move another muscle.

"Maybe."

CHAPTER TWENTY-TWO

GETTING THROUGH CUSTOMS in Jorwani took some time once they deplaned. The Jorwani authorities scrutinized their passports, staring at Cody and then his photo again and again until finally they were satisfied he was legit. Then they did the same thing to Miranda. She was placid while they did so, though Cody wanted to snap at the one dude who seemed to take a lot of pleasure in staring at Miranda's breasts rather than her face.

Finally they were through and hailing a taxi. The aid group was located in a neighborhood inside the capital city, Cape Lucier. Much of Cape Lucier was marked by the civil war that had raged for the past three years until Zain Okonjo overthrew the government and did his own cleansing of the population. Concrete buildings looked like swiss cheese in some places. In others, parts of buildings had crumbled from the fighting and lay in piles of broken cement and rebar. The streets were dusty and pockmarked with blast holes. The people looked fearful as they hurried about their daily business, women with baskets filled with whatever groceries they could beg, borrow, or steal and men with haunted looks that spoke of battle and bloodshed.

Cody knew that look, as did all Special Ops troops. They'd seen it far too many times before. The ratty taxi he and Miranda had taken from the airport dropped them off at the front of a compound that looked like every other building in the city. The sign out front proclaimed it was the Good Samaritan Aid Society. A bit cheeky considering that Jorwani was about ninety-percent Muslim. Another taxi belching fumes rocked to a halt and Kev MacDonald emerged with his wife in tow.

"Jesus, I was beginning to wonder if we'd make it," he said as he and Lucky walked over to where Cody stood with Miranda.

Lucky laughed. "We've ridden in worse, babe."

"True."

They walked in through the open gates of the compound. There was a truck inside, off-loading boxes, and a group of Jorwani citizens standing in a line waiting for whatever was in those boxes. The air smelled of dust and unwashed bodies, and the noise levels rose and fell as children cried and mothers tried to soothe them.

A man walked out of another building farther away and waved at them.

"Fucking hell," Kev said.

Cody snorted. "We knew it, didn't we? Where don't we go that Ian Black doesn't appear at some point?"

"Yeah, but still. I was hoping he was merely running this one from afar for a change."

"That's Ian Black?" Miranda asked, and Cody

glanced at her. He'd been trying not to make eye contact with her since the moment on the plane when she'd admitted that she wanted to suck his dick. Because holy hell, looking at her caused his blood pressure to spike. Something that felt very much like a growl hung deep in his throat, waiting for him to let it out. A growl like an animal made when it staked its claim on something.

Because he very much wanted to stake his claim on her. He was trying desperately not to think about all the ways he wanted to stake his claim since there wasn't going to be much opportunity for that kind of thing out here.

"Yeah, that's him. You know who he is?"

"I've heard of him."

Cody almost smiled at the lack of emotion in her voice. She'd probably been fed the standard CIA line about Black, which meant she didn't trust him. Not that she gave it away.

"Don't believe everything you hear. Black's an asshole, but he's been instrumental in a few things we've done."

Lucky turned and shot them a mischievous look. "Just wait until Nick and Victoria arrive. There might be a show."

"A show?" Miranda asked.

"Vic was working for Black when she and Nick hooked up. It was dicey, to say the least."

"Baby, I'm sure that's all in the past," Kev said.

Lucky shrugged. "We'll see."

"My, my," Black said as they approached. "The cat just keeps dragging the riffraff to my door today."

Lucky was unfazed by that statement as she sashayed forward and gave Black a hug. He shot Kev a look as he hugged her back. "Except for you, Lucky," he said. "Definitely not riffraff at all."

"Thanks, Ian. Love you too."

"Hands off my wife," Kev finally growled.

"And how are the marine animals today?" Black said as he let Lucky go, tipping his chin at Cody.

"Same as always. Ready to bite your fucking head off if necessary."

Black snorted a laugh. "God, I love you people. So uptight and angry for no reason. Hooyah!" His gaze narrowed in on Miranda. "Hello, Jane Wood," he said. "Been expecting you for a while."

Miranda arched an eyebrow, cool as ever. "I don't know why. Until yesterday, I had no plans to be here."

"You never know, do you?" Black stepped back. "All right, this reunion has been fun, but time's wasting. You aren't here for chitchat and neither am I. I'll show you to your accommodations. After that, you can come and see how the operation is run and maybe pitch in to help distribute aid to these people. The need is real, and we could use the bodies."

"That's not why you're here," Cody said, disputing the notion that Black had a big heart.

"No, it's not. But we help out because, first of all, these people need it. And second, it's a good source of intel on what's happening in the city."

He led them inside a long building that had a large room at one end and a central hallway with what appeared to be storerooms on either side. He reached one and swung the door open. "I've got three of these rooms for the couples since I assume you're working with your partner on something mission critical—unless you tell me differently, of course. The rest of the men will bunk in rooms of six. There's a meeting room in the back of the building that we use as a war room. It's secure—shielded from radio waves coming in or out—so it will suit your needs."

Cody peered into the room. It was no bigger than a closet back home really. There were two bunk beds against one wall and nothing else.

But it was private. He'd be in one of these with Miranda. Alone.

Holy hell.

Black left the door open and started down the hallway. "The other two rooms are here," he said, pointing as they passed. "And the bathroom is down here. There's only one shower—and there's no hot water, but you don't have to worry about that too much since it's basically tepid straight out of the pipes."

He stopped and turned to face them. "Chow's at five. It's nothing fancy, but it's not an MRE either."

"Thank God for that," Kev grumbled.

"Briefing tonight at twenty-two hundred in the war room after you've all arrived. That's where you'll know what we know about Okonjo and Conti. I'll leave you to do whatever it is you people do until then."

"Ian," Lucky called as he turned away.

"Yeah?"

"Are you any closer to finding whatever it is you're looking for?"

Cody didn't miss the way the man's eyes flattened for a second. There were rumors about Black, rumors that he was still on the CIA payroll, but nobody knew anything for sure. All they knew was that he seemed to be a law unto himself. A mercenary who worked for the highest bidder but always somehow seemed to be on the right side of things when the shit hit the fan.

Whatever was in his eyes faded, and Black shrugged dismissively. "I'm looking for decent work and profit for my people. I find that all the time."

"Well, I hope you continue to find it then," Lucky said softly.

He gave her a small smile and then turned and strode away.

"Hey, homies," a voice called and they turned to see a couple of Cody's teammates approaching. It was Camel who'd spoken. "Heard you were here."

"Just arrived. Find anything interesting?" Cody asked.

"Checked out the war room. It's sound. The gear is state of the art too. Black is certainly fitted out well."

"He's a mercenary," Kev said. "He doesn't have to file a requisition to get the goods."

They had the latest and greatest in HOT too, but Colonel Mendez fought hard for that. They all knew what it was like to be in outfits that had to make do with whatever they had. Improperly armored vehicles. Old computers. Gear that was good but not as good as it needed to be. Cody'd made a few field modifications to combat gear in his time, as they all had.

Being a SEAL was a fucking awesome deal any day of the week. Being a HOT SEAL was like being a SEAL on steroids. Fucking awesome with icing and a cherry on top.

He glanced at Miranda. She looked so damn pretty in her dress with the white cotton shirt tied over the top. She wasn't showing cleavage, but it was clear that her magnificent chest was holding the top of the dress up.

No wonder the Jorwani customs agent had spent so much time staring at her. Cody knew a sudden, overwhelming urge to drag her into the small room they were sharing and tug that dress down so he could suck those nipples into tight, hard points.

"All right, boys," Lucky said, cutting through the lustful haze in his mind. "Those people out there need help distributing supplies. I suggest we do that since that's why we're here for the next day or two."

"Let's put our bags away at least," Kev said only half-jokingly, and Cody recognized the look of a man who wanted some alone time with the woman he was crazy about.

Not that Cody was crazy about Miranda. He just wanted her. Right now would be a good time.

He dragged his gaze away from her and found that Lucky was watching him with narrowed eyes. It was as if she could tell what he was thinking. He barely resisted giving her a *who me?* look before she turned her gaze to her husband.

"We can take a few moments to freshen up. I'd say Jane and I need to change, of course. But no trying to distract me, Kev." She looked about as serious as bad news on a sunny day. "We'll meet out front in five minutes. Right?"

Nobody dared to disagree.

Miranda was used to hard work. She'd trained long and hard at the Farm, working to hone her body into a precision instrument. She was in the best shape of her life and had been for a few years now.

But slinging fifty-pound bags of rice and flour for a couple of hours used muscle groups she didn't know she possessed. By the time they finished helping to unload the trucks—another one had shown up while they worked—she was sore and tired and ready for a tepid shower.

Except she didn't have that luxury because her stomach was about to chew itself up from the inside out. She stopped and wiped the beads of sweat from her brow. She'd changed into a pair of lightweight cotton pants and a T-shirt. She'd brought a hat, thankfully, and she'd put that on to shade her face from the sun.

Miranda's gaze slipped to Cody. He'd removed his shirt some time ago, and her belly clenched at the sight of all that golden muscle. The other guys had removed their shirts too. Quite frankly, they were all magnificent. How couldn't they be considering what they did and how utterly in shape they had to be to do it?

She and Lucky were the only ones who didn't have the luxury of removing shirts in this heat, unfortunately.

"Is it time to eat yet?" Lucky asked, coming up beside her.

"God, I hope so. But I think I need to clean up first."

Lucky looked down at the sweat stains on her own clothes. "Yep, going to have to agree with you there."

"Think they'd notice if we snuck off?"

Lucky watched the men for a second. "Nah, probably not one of us. But if we both disappeared, oh yeah. You go ahead. I'll stay and cover for you."

Miranda felt like she should protest, but the truth was she didn't want to. She wanted to escape these larger-than-life men for a few minutes. Well, mostly *one* larger-than-life man. After what she'd said to him on the plane, after the revelation they were staying in a room together—a bunk room, but still a room—she had to take time to breathe and think. Were they headed where she thought they were headed? And could she handle it?

She could always ask Ian Black for another room if she didn't want to go there. Her mind immediately sent up an objection to that thought, however.

She arched her back and put a hand to the curve of her spine for a second. "Thanks," she said to Lucky. "I won't be long."

With one more glance at Cody, she headed for the building where their room lay. Thankfully there was AC, though it was anemic at best. But it did work to take some of the humidity out of the air.

Miranda gathered some fresh underwear and supplies and headed for the shower. The bathroom was old and creaky, with porcelain fixtures and a rust stain in the cast-iron tub that reminded her of her Granny's tub back in Alabama when Granny had still been alive.

For some insane reason, Miranda had liked to clean that rust spot. There was a certain cleanser, she couldn't think of the name of it now, but sprinkling it on and then scrubbing with a sponge was enough to make the rust magically disappear.

Maybe she'd enjoyed it because there was a tangible result to her hard work. It was something she'd been in control of, something that she could conquer.

She had half a thought that if she had that cleanser

here, she'd be down on her knees beside this tub, scrubbing the stain away. Instead, she turned and locked the door, then shed her clothes and turned on the tap. The water trickled out at a steady pace and, yeah, it was tepid. No such thing as a hot shower here, but at least it wasn't cold either.

Miranda stepped under the spray and washed off the sweat and dirt of the day. She worked quickly because it was obvious the water wasn't precisely plentiful. When she finished, she grabbed one of the pitiful, threadbare towels stacked on a table nearby and dried as much as she could before tugging on clothing against damp skin.

Then she gathered her things and jerked open the door, intending to rush back to her room and go spell Lucky so she could have a shower too.

But instead of an empty hallway, she came face-to-face with a large, bare-chested man with blue eyes. The sight of him punched her in the gut the way it always did and left her gasping for air. She only prayed she didn't do something idiotic, like swoon because her knees gave out.

"I'm disappointed in you, Jane," Cody drawled, lifting his arms to grasp the doorframe, effectively preventing her escape.

"Uhh, why?"

His gaze did that slow crawl down her body that always heated her up from the inside out.

"Because you didn't wait for me."

CHAPTER TWENTY-THREE

MIRANDA'S MOUTH FELL open for a second before she seemed to catch herself and snapped it shut. For Miranda, that was a pretty big reaction. Cody knew she'd be pissed at herself for showing him that much. He resisted the urge to push her back inside the bathroom and lock the door behind them.

But only barely.

He grinned at her and then dropped one hand and stepped aside, letting her escape if she so chose. She didn't move. Green eyes that weren't hers watched him evenly. Her hair was wet and slick against her head, putting the emphasis on the planes of her face. She had delicately arched brows, creamy skin, and a finely carved nose set above full lips and a firm chin. She looked delicate and too pretty to be useful, but he knew that none of that was true.

Miranda Jane wasn't delicate or useless. She was beautiful and lethal. And sexier than fuck, damn her.

He'd had no intention of going there with her again.

He'd only wanted to stop Cash-Money from getting there—but hell, after that conversation with her earlier, it was pretty much all he could think about. Her mouth on his dick. His mouth on her pussy. His cock sinking into her sweet body as her eyes dilated and her lips fell open with pleasure.

Her breaths and moans as he began to move. The way her fingers curled hard into his arms and then harder into his shoulders before slipping to his ass and gripping that too. Her hips lifting as she slammed against him, trying to take him deeper.

Damn, it had been good with her. So good that he hadn't fucked anyone since that night. Of course, he'd never thought he'd get to fuck her again. But he could. She was going to let him. He could see it in her eyes, in the pulse that throbbed wildly in her neck. She was his for the taking.

And he was going to take her. Every which way he wanted, damn her. Every which way that made her beg him for more. And then he was going to walk away and never think about her again.

If that hurt her feelings, well, she deserved it. Not that he thought she had any feelings to hurt really.

"There's not enough water," she said.

"Not enough for what?"

"Not enough to shower together."

"Honey, I'd think showering together would save water."

She nibbled her lower lip, and he had to work not to groan. "Not if we lost track of time."

"True." He stepped into her space, breathed in the clean scent of her skin. "If you're in the room when I get done, you'd better be naked."

Her eyes widened and her mouth dropped open just slightly. It wasn't shock he saw there. It was desire. Her gaze swept his body quickly, and then she stepped out of the doorway to let him inside. She was clutching her dirty clothing to her chest like a shield. He doubted she realized it.

"You planning to be there, Jane?" he asked softly as he backed into the bathroom.

"I don't know."

He shrugged as he trailed a lazy hand down his torso. "Your choice as to when—but make no mistake, it *will* happen eventually."

For the first time, she stiffened slightly. "You seem so certain. Am I that easy to read?"

He started to tell her yeah, it was precisely that, but something stopped him. Instead, he told her the truth. "We both are. There's something that won't let us stay away, something deep inside that drives us to seek pleasure in each other. We're like magnet and metal, water and life, yin and yang. Something in you needs something in me—and it's the same for me. It's probably only temporary, but it's right now—and neither of us is going to deny that part of ourselves any longer. Are we?"

He was almost as surprised as she was by his words. He'd said more than he'd intended, that was for sure.

It took her a long moment to respond, but she shook her head. "I don't intend to deny anything."

***

Miranda didn't know what she was doing. She stood in the room she was sharing with Cody, her heart tripping in her chest, her back to the door as she waited with arms folded over her body and stared out the small window set high in the wall. All she could see was sky, but that was enough. It was blue, so blindingly blue it would hurt if she was outside and looking up without the protection being inside provided. A white cloud drifted lazily across the sky like a ship on the ocean. It was beautiful and sad at the same time.

Why sad, Miranda? Why?

Because it made her feel her loneliness so acutely. The sky had always made her feel lonely and restless. Maybe it was crazy, but when she'd been a girl, she'd stared up into that sky, that bright blue Alabama sky with the haze of heat shimmering over it, and felt like she didn't belong. Like there was so much more to life and she didn't know how to find it.

The sky made her dream. And her dreams were never enough, never quite right. She'd never yet found what she wanted, what made her feel safe and complete.

So why was she standing here, waiting for a man who had the power to wreck whatever peace of mind she had?

Because Cody had that power. She didn't know why or how, but he did. He'd said there was something between them, something that drew them like metal and magnets, something in her that needed something in him.

It made her shudder at just how right he was. Because something in her did need him. She came alive when he was near. Deep down, she felt an excitement she hadn't felt in years. A desire to love and be loved.

No. Absolutely not. Stop this.

She didn't trust love. Never had. Her parents hadn't loved her or her sisters enough to stop being the broken, selfish people they were. Mark hadn't loved her the way she'd wanted. If anything, he'd loved her like a friend, like a buddy who made you feel happy and comfortable but not as if your skin might split if you didn't do something with all the feelings your body contained.

Feelings. What crazy things they were. How they'd gotten so tangled up over a man she hardly knew was beyond her. But he excited her and made her feel hopeful—a thing she thought she'd forgotten.

The door swung open behind her and her skin prickled. She didn't turn. She didn't need to. It was him. She could *feel* him. His presence called to her, gave off heat and so much magnetism she thought she might burn up in the pull of it.

"You aren't naked," he growled.

She didn't turn. "No, I'm not."

She felt him move rather than heard him. And then she felt him behind her, so big and beautiful and solid. A protector. A dangerous, hardened SEAL warrior.

His hands settled on her shoulders, ran down her arms and then went around her waist, tugging her back against his hard body. His mouth dipped to her ear, and shivers ran down her spine and into the warm, wet recesses of her body.

"But you're still here."

"I am."

His tongue flicked her earlobe and she gasped. Then his lips were on her neck, his tongue gliding over her flesh. "Do you want me, Miranda Jane?" he breathed against her skin.

"You know the answer."

"I want you to say it. I need to hear it."

"I want you, Cody," she forced out past the lump

gathering in her throat. God, why was she so emotional with him? Why did he drag things from the depths of her soul that no man ever had?

She thought he might turn her in his arms. And if he did, she might lose it. She might sob with the emotion choking her.

But he didn't. As if he knew she needed the time to process this thing between them, he did not make a move to face her. Instead, his hands went to her breasts, cupping them, his fingers finding and tweaking the stiff nipples beneath the fabric of her shirt.

Her body was on fire. Lightning streaked beneath her skin, popping and sizzling and sparking until she was on edge.

"Such beautiful breasts," he murmured. "So sensitive."

He reached for the buttons of her shirt, deftly slipping them free as he stood behind her, his body crowding hers in the best way. And then he slipped the shirt from her shoulders. When his fingers went beneath her bra straps and tugged them down, she didn't protest. His mouth was on her shoulder, licking and kissing her skin as he unsnapped her bra and pulled that free as well.

Then his big hands cupped her breasts, bare skin to bare skin. When he tugged her back against him this time, she felt the hard bulge of his cock in the small of her back and she shuddered.

"Kiss me, Miranda," he said, and she shifted slightly to the side, tilted her head back, and met his mouth. It was as if someone set off an incendiary bomb. The fire exploding in her body was immediate and intense. Cody groaned as their tongues met. She tried to turn, tried to get better access, but he held her in place, devoured her mouth this way, drinking her in while she drowned in him.

"Cody," she gasped when he finally let her breathe.

He spun her in his arms this time. "Goddamn, sunshine," he said, "you make me ache. You make me willing to walk on hot coals just for a taste of you."

She slipped her arms around his neck and pulled herself closer to him. "You don't have to walk on hot coals. Just— God, just fuck me, okay? Make this stop. Make it better."

"I wanted to do this differently," he growled, "but I need to be in you. Now."

"Yes, please. Please now," she begged.

She reached for his pants at the same time he did. And then his hands were on hers, holding them tight. He swore. "No condoms, baby. *Shit.*"

She blinked. "It doesn't matter, Cody. I get birth control shots. And you're the only man I've had sex with in over a year."

He was looking at her with a sort of stunned expression. What if he didn't believe her? What if he said no?

"I never fuck without a condom. Never."

She put her hand on his cheek and smiled even though she wanted to cry inside. "It's okay. I understand. We'll find another way."

He blinked. And then he laughed before he started to unbutton his pants again. "No, baby, no way. I was just telling you that I'm safe. That you don't have to worry. But I'm going in there. If you really want that, I'm going in bare. I want to feel you wrapped around me."

Heat pulsed through her. "I definitely want that. You have no idea."

He shoved his pants down his hips at the same time she divested herself of hers. Then he bent to lift her up, gripping her bare ass in his big hands. She automatically put her legs around his waist. A second later, his cock was there, nudging into her slick heat. Miranda wiggled until she was in a better position and then sank down on him until they both groaned.

"Oh God," she said as he slid home.

"Too much?" he asked worriedly.

"No. No way. Just feels so amazing." And it did. Her heart was out of control, zooming like a fighter jet on a mission, and her skin prickled with heat. She felt so full of him. Perfectly, wonderfully full.

"I couldn't wait," he said, his voice deep and growly in that way she loved. "Need you too much."

"Then don't wait."

He lifted her up and then plunged her down again and again on his cock. Miranda grasped his face in her hands and fused her mouth to his. Their joining was hard and almost violent, but in a good way. Violently good as he rocked into her over and over, his cock splitting her just right, rubbing against all the nerves in her G-spot. She moaned. He moaned. She wasn't sure who made what noise, but they both did as he moved even faster inside her.

Her world tilted abruptly, and she found herself on her back on the lower bunk, Cody looming over her like a mountain of muscle, his cock still deep inside her. If it had been perfect before, it was even better now. He hooked her knees wide and drove into her. She was so close, so unbearably close to shattering into a million pieces.

He thrust again, and as if he'd flipped a switch, all the pressure inside her detonated. Her orgasm rolled through her like a wave, obliterating everything in its path. The aftershocks reverberated into her limbs, her toes, sapping her of strength and reason.

He came soon after, warm liquid filling her as he shot himself deep inside her. They were both breathing hard when he lifted his head to look down at her. He looked about as confused as she felt. She held her breath, wondering if he would leave her now. And then she got brave and lifted her fingers to his lips, tracing them softly.

"I still want more," she said, and he shuddered, his cock still inside her, still hard.

"So do I." His brows drew together for a second. "I don't understand this. But I'm not ready to stop."

"Then we won't."

CHAPTER TWENTY-FOUR

IT WAS EASY to say they wouldn't stop, and yet they had to at some point. But not before they frantically joined their bodies again. Though, to be technical about it, they never quite unjoined.

Cody was still hard, still deep inside her, when he rolled to the side and took her with him. She put a leg over his waist, giving him access as they lay face-to-face. It was incredibly intimate, though he tried not to think about that part. This was about fucking. About feeling good for the sake of feeling good.

He hadn't forgiven her. He might never forgive her. But holy hell, he was going to enjoy her.

He flexed his body, driving his cock into her wet heat, and she gasped at the same time that he felt her entire body shudder around him.

"You like that?"

"You know I do." Her arms were around his neck, her fingers stealing into his hair. He wanted to kiss her, but he also wanted to look at her. Wanted to watch her face as he made her come.

"I want to see your eyes," he said.

She bit her lip. "You are seeing them."

"No. *Your* eyes. Not these contacts."

"I have to take them out at night."

He didn't know why that made him happy, but it did. Logically, he knew she was the same woman. She felt the same. Tasted the same. Sounded the same. And, yeah, mostly looked the same. But he loved her golden eyes, loved all that cascading blond hair. Though red was hot. He had to admit it was.

He thrust hard into her and she moaned, grasping him tight. He wanted to brand her. Wanted to make her his. At least for now, at least while this heat and need raged inside him like a fire.

A few days from now, he wouldn't care. Then she could fuck Money and he wouldn't even give a damn.

"Cody… yes, like that. Oh, yes…"

He slipped his hand between them, found her sweet spot. He wanted to lick that pussy so badly, but it would have to wait until later. Instead, he manipulated her with his fingers while driving deep into her heat, fucking her slowly and thoroughly for as long as he could.

Which wasn't long. The pressure built in his balls, driving him to move harder and faster and more desperately. They rolled as one until she was on her back again, her legs wrapped high around his waist, her body opening to him even more. He took her mouth, devoured her as he fucked her like it was the last time he'd ever fuck anyone.

And hell, maybe it was. This job was dangerous. Not that he went downrange with the thought that he wasn't coming back, but it was always a possibility. For all of them.

Except he couldn't lose her again. Not yet. And not like he had before, when he'd thought she was dead. He had too much he wanted to do to her yet, too many things he wanted to explore. He didn't know why he was compelled to claim her, but he simply was. It was a need that would burn itself out in a few days. Two weeks tops, he told himself.

Their bodies were in sync this time, rising to the top of the mountain together and then plunging off the peak and into the valley below. It was a helluva rush, coming inside her in a way he'd never come in another woman in his life. Bare skin to bare skin, his semen filling her.

This time they collapsed and lay together, breathing hard. He was sweating. She was too. The air wasn't cool enough in the room, but he wouldn't change what they'd just done so they could be more comfortable.

She turned her head to look at him, those green eyes both sad and content at the same time.

"Just so you know," she said softly. "It's still not enough."

Getting naked with Cody wasn't a good idea at all, and yet she'd do it again in a heartbeat. After they'd recovered from the second frantic session they'd had, they'd gotten out of bed, gotten dressed, and then she went to the common dining area ten minutes before he planned to arrive.

He'd kissed her and she'd melted into him, willing to get naked one more time if he wanted it.

But then her stomach growled, and he laughed as he pushed her away. "Food, Miranda Jane," he said. "Then sex."

"More sex," she corrected.

"As much as you can handle," he said, a twinkle in his eye as he opened the bedroom door.

She'd left him standing there, her pulse humming crazily as she walked away. She could feel his eyes on her, and she'd wanted to turn and go back to him for some insane reason.

But she didn't. She nibbled her lip as she made her way through the compound. Yes, they'd had sex, and yes, he'd been a fantastic lover, making sure she felt as good as he did. But he'd been so angry with her earlier that she didn't think that kind of anger went away in a few hours' time. Not even for sex.

They were experiencing a détente, nothing more. She prayed it ended in peace, but she didn't think it would.

Which is why you need to enjoy it while you can.

Miranda found the dining room, a rectangular room with three long tables and a small buffet line at one side. She went to the line, got her dinner—some sort of vegetable soup with goat meat and a huge hunk of local flatbread—and then headed toward where Lucky sat with her husband. The other woman's eyebrows quirked as she approached. Lucky broke off a piece of bread and popped it into her mouth.

"Everything okay?" she asked brightly after Miranda

sat down.

She tried not to wince as her bottom met the hard bench seat. She ached, but in a good way. In an oh-my-God-I-am-doing-this-again-as-soon-as-possible way. Yes, she was a little sore. And no, she wasn't intending to stop. It was somewhat like being a virgin again, though not quite so bad.

"Everything's fine. How about you?"

Lucky grinned as she shot a look at Kev. "Oh yes. Most definitely fine. Couldn't be better."

"Sorry I didn't make it back outside to give you a chance at the shower."

Lucky shrugged and then winked. "It's okay. It worked out." Her smile widened as she gazed at something over Miranda's shoulder. "Well, well. Doesn't Cowboy look relaxed?"

Miranda ate her soup and kept her mouth shut. No way was she falling for the bait. A few minutes later, a heavy form plopped down beside her on the bench. She didn't have to look at him to know it was Cody. She could feel his presence like it was her own.

"Feeling better, Cowboy?" Lucky asked.

Cody stilled from whatever he was doing. Miranda didn't know because she wasn't going to look at him. "A shower will do wonders for a guy. Or maybe it was the nap I took after."

"A nap. Sure, why not?"

Miranda turned to look at him—because she decided that deliberately avoiding him was more of a red flag than trying to make conversation—and her heart did that little hitch thing it always did.

"Is that your team name? Cowboy?"

He gave her a look filled with heat and infinite possibility. "Yep, that's it."

"You never told me that back in the desert," she said, and his brows drew down as if she were in danger of imparting information the others might not know. "Oh, it's okay." She nodded at Lucky. "She guessed the truth."

"Yep," Lucky said, relishing what she was saying perhaps a little too much. "You were in such a bad mood when Jane showed up that Vic and I put two and two together."

"I'm still in a bad mood," he said, tearing off a piece of bread oh so casually. "But we have a job to do, and I'm not going to let it bother me. But Jane's not planning on performing any death scenes again… are you, Jane?"

Miranda swallowed. "Not on purpose. Any death scenes this time will be real, I assure you."

"Oh God, I hope not," Lucky said, sounding horrified. "No death scenes from anyone. That's an order."

Kev laughed at his wife as he put an arm around her. "You aren't in a position to give orders, babe."

She put a hand on his cheek and smiled at him. "I could be… later tonight."

Envy blossomed in Miranda's chest. It was obvious these two were in love. Incredible, deep, soul-mate love. She wanted to know what that was like, and yet she didn't think she ever would.

She had a terrible penchant for picking the wrong man, apparently. Mark. A couple of lovers who hadn't lasted. Cody, a man who no doubt hated her deep down but had no problem setting that issue aside so he could gratify urges he probably wished he didn't have.

She had no illusions about what was going on between them. It was sex, pure and simple. Maybe she was crazy for indulging, but if life had taught her anything it was to seize the day and take whatever happiness she could find for however long it lasted.

Because, in her experience, it never lasted long. Something always came along and ripped it away, whether it was life or a bomb or just the fading of illusions.

Ian Black entered the room and headed for their table. When he sat down next to her, she didn't shrink from his gaze. Cody might have made a noise beside her, but she didn't look at him.

"You're still missing five of your operators," he said as he flicked a hard gaze over them all.

"We don't have control of the flight schedules," Cody drawled.

"No, but I'm getting reports that Conti might move location sooner than expected."

"Is he going with Okonjo?" Miranda asked. Mendez had said that the Kenyan authorities issued a warrant for Conti's arrest, but that didn't mean he hadn't found a way around it. God knew the man was good at greasing the right palms. It's how he'd stayed a step ahead of all the traps that had been set for him over the years.

"No," Black said. "But there's a ship in the harbor—a ship that holds a cargo no one is talking about. And it's scheduled to sail in three days. My sources say Conti plans to be on it."

"They'll be here soon," Lucky said.

"Even if they aren't," Cody cut in, "we've got this. Infiltrating a ship is what we do. It's what we're trained for."

"You're going to have to plan for two infiltrations,"

Ian replied. "One at the palace and one at the ship. Hopefully we'll know where he is by go time, but if not, you'll be splitting up. Still think you don't need those extra bodies? Not to mention the best sniper I've ever known… and her husband," he added, though Miranda would have said that part was added reluctantly.

And then she processed what she'd just heard. Victoria was a sniper, and apparently a damned good one. Whoa. She wasn't a bad marksman herself, but snipers were a different breed. The patience required—and the distance skills—were incredible.

She frowned as she thought about what else Black had said. Two missions. Two infiltrations. Two possible locations for Conti. Of course, because nothing about Victor Conti had ever been easy.

"I thought you were some sort of badass know-it-all," Kev drawled in a heavy Southern accent that reminded her of home. "You're supposed to have concrete intel as to which location we'll find the bastard."

The other SEALs had stopped talking and were listening to the conversation. The guys from Alpha Squad were as well.

Ian Black sighed. "As usual, you ungrateful motherfuckers want the world. I'm giving you the best I got. Jorwani is not my primary territory, and I've got fewer sources here than elsewhere. We're working on it, but good sources are hard to come by—sources I can *trust,* that is."

"Conti will go to the ship," Miranda said, and every eye in the place turned to look at her. But she knew the man and she knew what she was talking about. "He's not the sort of man to stay under another's thumb, especially a dictator like Okonjo. He's got his own people, his own empire. He'll go because there's something he's moving on that ship. Weapons. Contraband. Women."

"Jesus Christ," one of the men muttered.

She felt the sting of that comment, but she wasn't going to back down. "You don't have to believe me," she said coolly. "I only spent about six months learning the man's life and turning myself into the sort of woman he'd deal with."

"That's not what he meant," Cody murmured.

"I believe you," the same man said. A dark-haired man with a slight accent. Who was he again? Oh yes, Matt was his name. Matt Girard. She didn't recall his team name. "Wasn't suggesting I didn't. Just fucking disgusted at the idea he's trafficking women."

Miranda drew in a deep breath. She wasn't used to having a team, as she'd told Cody before. She was used to fighting and scrapping for every bit of ground she gained.

"My mistake."

"Nah, don't worry about it. My fault for not being clearer." He stood up at the same time the man she'd heard the others call Viking did. "Looks like we'd better get busy planning two missions, brother," Matt said to Viking.

The other man nodded. "Roger that. Let's get that motherfucker and put a stop to his operations."

CHAPTER TWENTY-FIVE

THEY MET IN Ian Black's war room. It was secure, a smaller room surrounded by a metal cage inside a bigger room, which meant nobody could pick up any transmissions. Both teams were there, with the exception of their five missing operators who were arriving later tonight.

"My source says he's still in the palace," Ian Black said. "But Okonjo isn't leaving for two more days, and Conti could have moved by then. I've got people watching the gates, but it won't be easy to tell who's coming and going."

"Anybody watching the ship?" Viking asked.

"I've got a guy… but it would be better if you put one of yours on it."

"All right. What about weapons and gear? We'll need dive gear if we're going to infiltrate a ship. We also need Rapid Diver systems."

"I've got what you need. It's military grade, though not all of it's strictly American, if you know what I mean."

"Comm?" Cody interjected. Because that shit was important too.

"Just like you use back home," Black said with a grin. He walked over to the computer and brought up a map of the presidential palace that appeared on the monitor. "Conti is here," he said, pointing to a room in the east wing of the vast palace. It was an exterior room, which was even better for them because it would make grabbing him easier if they had multiple points of entry. A point right into his room? Bonus.

"How do you know?" Money asked.

"Multiple reports place him there at night. Conti likes the ladies, and he's had several brought to him in this room during his stay. They spend the night, sometimes more than one at a time, and then go on their way the next morning. The local madams have been delighted with his appetite for women. Always new ones, never the same girl twice. It's noticeable, which is good for us. And the madams are happy to let the girls tell my people where they were taken."

"If he's bringing in women, why not send one of us in to take him down? I could neutralize him before these guys show up and extract us."

Cody gaped at Miranda. Instantly, everything inside him went still. "No," he snapped before anyone could agree. It was a stupid idea. A dangerous idea. And he needed some reason other than he couldn't stand the thought of her in danger. "He's seen her," he added, looking at his teammates. "She looks different than she did then, sure, but it wouldn't take him long to realize she's the same woman."

Miranda arched an eyebrow. "You don't know that.

He doesn't look at women twice. Well, at least not their faces. If the tits and ass are there, that's all he cares about. He'll glance at me, and then he'll want me on my knees with my mouth wrapped around his dick."

Anger swelled inside him like a tidal wave. The idea of her on her knees in front of anyone but him was enough to make him want to commit violence. "And how far would you let it go before you neutralized him?"

Her brows drew down. It was an indication of just how pissed she was because Miranda was usually damned good at masking her emotions. "As far as I have to in order to take him down," she snapped. "Which wouldn't be far. A hand on his balls and it's over."

Lucky snorted, and Cody tried not to glare at all of them for refusing to take this seriously.

"Good God, don't remind us," one of the Alpha Squad guys said. "Every time I think of that night, I sweat."

Lucky grinned. "Sorry, Ice."

"In case y'all are wondering," Kev said to the SEALs, "my sweet wife took down the world's most wanted terrorist with an application of, uh, pressure to his balls."

"So it works," Lucky said. "Which all of us in this room know. And Cowboy?"

He looked directly at her because he knew she was waiting for him to do it.

"That wasn't a fair question of a fellow operator, and you know it."

He felt the sting of that statement. "No, probably not. But Jane here is CIA. And I've seen the lengths they're willing to go to."

Miranda knew what he meant. That statement hung in

the air between them like a poisonous cloud until she cleared her throat and drew everyone's attention back to her. "Nevertheless, it's still a good plan. Send one of the women in as a prostitute. I'll volunteer since I'm sure Lucky and Victoria are needed in other capacities."

"It's a bad idea," Cody said, trying to remain reasonable about the whole thing. "You don't need to go in. We can do the fucking job without you taking that risk."

"Enough," Viking said. "Can we get on with this? You two can argue later. And Jane," he added, "that's not a bad plan. We'll put it into rotation. If we're lucky, it won't be necessary and we'll get to him another way. But thanks for volunteering."

"Whatever it takes," Miranda said, her voice sounding firm and determined.

But Cody was equally determined that it wasn't going to happen. They'd just have to see which of them won the battle.

Miranda knew Cody was pissed at her, but there was nothing she could do about it right then. They spent the next hour discussing plans to infiltrate both the palace and the ship. Ian Black didn't have a schematic of the ship yet, but he was working on it. Still, it seemed as if the SEALs already knew what they'd find. It was a cargo ship, but what Conti was shipping was anybody's guess—though it wasn't likely to be good. Especially considering the money he'd been sending to Okonjo for the past month or so.

He could be buying guns, sure. He could also by buying something far worse. Nuclear material. Chemical weaponry, which Okonjo possessed because he'd used it on his people. Or he could be buying human beings, which was the most disgusting choice of all and yet also very likely.

Victor Conti had made pornographic films back in Vegas, but he was also suspected of engaging in sex trafficking. As if the films weren't enough. As if the young women willing to let their bodies be bought for the price of drugs or, hell, just the chance at a certain kind of fame weren't enough for his operation. He'd made money off those films. When was it enough?

The meeting wrapped up, and everyone headed for the storerooms where Ian Black had the weapons and gear. Miranda didn't go with them. Instead, she went outside and stood in the courtyard, listening to the traffic moving outside the walls. It was steady, though not fast. The rubble and general state of disrepair in this part of Cape Lucier dictated that.

She could hear a dog barking and then a woman yelling at someone. A child cried. There were cooking smells in the air, and the smell of decay as well. Cape Lucier wasn't a pleasant place, though it had once been. That's what happened when warlords took control and did what they pleased.

It disgusted her. It's what she fought against, what she would always fight against. Stopping the world's assholes from destroying everything good.

She started to turn and head back inside when a shape appeared out of the darkness. It was a large shape and adrenaline surged in her veins as her fight response kicked in—but then the man moved closer and Cody materialized in front of her. She could feel his confusion and his anger. She didn't want to disappoint him or upset him, but this wasn't about what she wanted. It was about what was right for the mission.

"What are you doing out here?" he asked.

"Thinking."

"There's a lot to think about."

"There always is." She folded her arms, hugging herself. "We do what we do because we have to. It's the same for both of us."

"Yeah, that's true. But sunshine, you don't have to risk yourself. We'll get the bastard without you putting yourself in danger."

She didn't bother to point out that he'd be putting himself in danger—that they all would—in order to get Conti in the first place. "Ideally, yes. But shouldn't we be prepared for every possibility? Women are a weakness for him—don't tell me you didn't think of this solution the first moment Black said he'd been using prostitutes. All of you did."

He hesitated too long. "It's not what we do. The CIA might send you in to play a fucking madam or porn purveyor or whatever, but it's not the way we operate. We don't *need* to operate that way. And we don't involve noncoms in our missions."

She sighed. "Cody, I'm not a noncombatant. I'm an agent. I've been in plenty of battles, though not the same sort of battles you fight. But I still volunteered to put myself in harm's way for the sake of my nation. Could you please stop acting like you're the only soldier here?"

"Sailor," he said.

She blinked. Oh yeah, Navy. She'd forgotten for a second.

"Well, I'm not a sailor and never have been. But I'm definitely a soldier. Just not the kind who wears a uniform. So stop trying to protect me. I can protect myself."

He blew out a breath like he was patiently trying to explain his obviously superior position to an idiot. Her hackles rose. Damn stubborn man!

"I can't help it," he said, his tone no longer superior but sounding tired instead. The anger rising within her subsided just a little bit. Like blowing cool air on a pot of boiling water. She was still angry, but not in danger of boiling over just yet.

"Try, Cowboy. Try to realize I'm your equal, even if you can't quite comprehend it."

"I keep thinking about that day," he said. "You were lying in the dirt, blood spilling everywhere, and all I could think was that I'd failed you. Fucking let them kill you when I'd sworn I wouldn't."

Her throat tightened and her chest felt as if someone had punched her and left a hole. If she could change that moment— But God, she couldn't. "I'm sorry."

"I know. But I still see it—and I still believe it in some ways. Not that you actually died, but that you could—and if you did, it would be my fault."

She swallowed. "No, it would be mine. Never yours."

He raked a hand over his scalp. "That's easy for you to say. But you didn't live with it the way I did."

She took a step forward and then stopped. "I know that Conti sent men after you. I know that's because of me, because you helped me. Do you think for one second I won't do everything I can to prevent them from harming *you?*"

He seemed a bit stunned at first. And then he moved toward her, only stopping when he was right in front of her. Part of her wished he'd take her in his arms, but part of her was scared too. There was something going on inside her, something that made her feel a little bit crazy and a little bit jumpy all at once.

"We'll get Conti. He's not going to hurt me—but if you go in there and I have to worry about you— Not a good thing for me, sunshine."

Miranda stared up into those blue, blue eyes, but she wasn't expecting what happened next. She wasn't expecting her heart to crack wide open or a tumult of feelings to race through her. Nobody cared what happened to her the way he did. Nobody tried to stop her from doing her job because they were scared *for* her. Mark, Badger, Sam. They'd never expressed this level of concern for her.

Hell, her parents had never expressed this level of concern either.

Whoa there, Miranda. Doesn't mean anything. Doesn't mean this man wants to tie any knots or have babies with you.

"Why do you care?" she asked, her voice raspy with emotion she couldn't stuff down. "Why does it matter to you what happens to me?"

"I don't know," he said, and her stomach fell to her toes.

Well, what had she expected?

She refused to let her disappointment show. "It's okay. I was just wondering."

She started to push past him and head for the room

they shared, but he grabbed her and spun her around, pulling her into his arms. She closed her eyes as she gripped his shoulders, put her nose against his chest, and breathed in the scent of him.

Spicy, sweaty, masculine. Cody.

Her heart hurt as she stood there. Physically hurt. She felt so much with him, so very much. He was hell on her emotions, especially now when she wanted him to say he cared but all he'd said was *I don't know*. Why had he gotten to her? He was just a man she'd abducted in a casino so she could escape Victor Conti. A random stranger—and now he was in her system so deep she didn't think she'd ever get him out.

"That's a lie," he said, his voice low and rumbling in her ear. "I care because I like you, Miranda."

Those words were hot and bright and beautiful. They meant something to her, even if they were fairly ordinary. Her blood rushed in her veins, and her chest swelled with everything she was trying to contain. She liked him too. Maybe more than liked him. Not that she understood what any of that meant, but this was definitely more than like on her part.

"I like you too," she said because she couldn't say anything else. How could she put into words what she was feeling when even she didn't understand it?

"Don't take any unnecessary risks. That's all I ask."

Her throat tightened. "Same goes for you, Cowboy."

CHAPTER TWENTY-SIX

FUCKING HELL, THEY weren't even a real couple and they were already fighting. Logically, he knew Miranda was tough and capable of taking care of herself. But he didn't have to like it, and he damned sure didn't have to like the idea of her offering herself as bait to get to Victor Conti. He stood there with her in his arms, asking himself just exactly what he thought he was doing. She pushed away first. He wanted to reach for her and drag her back, but he didn't.

"It's getting late," she said.

"Yeah."

"Did you get all the equipment you need?"

"Black is remarkably well equipped. Yeah, we'll be fine."

"I guess I should get a weapon or two. Maybe some body armor."

She said it lightly, but he could tell she was just talking for the hell of it. Stalling. Was she telling him without saying it that sex wasn't happening again? He didn't really know because he'd never actually cared before. If a woman he was sleeping with decided to withhold sex for some reason, that was his cue to move on. He didn't have time for that shit—and it wasn't going to get him to commit to a relationship, which was usually the intent of such things.

He didn't know what she was saying, but if that's where she was going with it then he'd adapt. He wouldn't like it, but he'd adapt.

"You aren't required to sleep with me, Miranda. One and done is fine if that's what you want."

"I wasn't… Where did you… Is that what you want?"

He processed that confusing garble of words and picked out the important bit to him. "No, it's not what I want."

"It's not what I want either. I thought I made that clear."

"You could've changed your mind."

"Because you don't want me to act as bait to Conti?" She shook her head, her hair sliding like silk against her shoulders. "I'd like to think I'm smart enough to separate the job from the personal side. Though I guess if I was really smart, I'd save the personal side for when the job is done and Conti's in custody."

He lifted an eyebrow. "Are you feeling smart tonight?"

She grinned and it hit him in the chest like the recoil from a grenade launcher. God, she was pretty. And she touched something inside him that he didn't think had ever been touched before.

"I'm feeling exceedingly stupid. Reckless even. I don't want to save a thing for later. I want it all right now."

That was all he needed to hear. He took her hand and led her inside. The halls were mostly empty, but no one stopped them as they passed. Money stepped out of the bunk room he was sharing with the guys and then leaned back against the door as they passed, smirking knowingly.

Cody refrained from wiping the smirk off his face, but only barely.

"Lucky bastard," Money said after Cody ushered Miranda into the room they shared and turned to shut the door. He didn't think she heard it because she'd gone over to where she'd put her bag and started rifling through it. But he did. He gave Money what he hoped was a quelling look. Yeah, they often trash-talked about sleeping with women, but the last thing he wanted was any trash talk about Miranda.

Money held up both hands. "Copy that loud and clear, Cowboy." Then he headed down the hall toward the bathroom, whistling a tune Cody didn't bother to figure out before he shut the door and faced Miranda.

"Strip," she said.

"You first."

She raised an eyebrow. "Same time."

"Copy." He reached for the bottom of his T-shirt and yanked it up and over his head. By the time he got out of everything, she was just shimmying out of her panties. She dropped them to the floor, and he thought he'd never seen anything more perfect in his life.

He reached for her, but she stepped away. "No. I know what happens when you get your hands on me—and I want my chance to taste you first. Promise you'll let me."

He could tell her no way in hell was he standing still for what she wanted to do, but he lied instead. He'd let her taste, but that was it. "All right."

She glided toward him, hips swaying, breasts bouncing with each step, and he thought he might die right there from how the sight of her affected him. His cock was harder than steel. Anticipation rushed through his veins. His brain was rapidly losing its ability to think complicated thoughts.

There was one thought: *this, now.*

When she reached out and took his cock in her hand, he thought he would never feel such perfection as her hand on him again.

"Oh, Cody—the things you do to me. The way you make me feel," she whispered before putting her soft lips on his chest, gliding her tongue over his pecs and then taking a nipple in her mouth.

He let his head fall back, forced himself to endure while she licked her way down his torso. And then she was kneeling before him, holding him in both hands, and he looked down into those eyes that were hers but not hers—and something rocked him hard, squeezing the breath from his lungs as he met her gaze for long moments. He had the craziest idea in that moment that he would do anything—*anything*—to keep her.

"You are so gorgeous," she said before sliding her tongue along the underside of his cock, her eyes still locked on his.

Mad need rolled through him. Just as she made the trip back up to the tip and closed her lips on him, he reached down and pulled her up.

"What are you doing?"

"This," he told her, tugging her over to the bed and lying back on it. She started to climb onto the bed with him, but he stopped her. “The other way,” he urged. “Knees up here.”

It took her a second but she figured out what he wanted, putting her knees on either side of his head and bending over to take his cock in her mouth again. Within seconds, she shuddered as he touched his tongue to her clit, the moan in her throat vibrating against his dick.

He licked her mercilessly until she couldn’t suck him anymore, until she had to wrench her mouth free so she could breathe as she came hard against his tongue, her hips jerking in little circles as she panted and moaned his name.

“I hate you,” she said when she was spent, collapsing against his torso, still breathing hard. “You never let me do what I want to you.”

“Mmm, and I love this view,” he told her. “I could look at your pussy all day. You’re so wet for me, Miranda.”

“I wanted to make you feel good.”

“You definitely do, honey. I feel real good.”

She sighed. “You can’t help but take control, can you?”

“Nope. Now do you wanna keep talking or do you want to fuck?”

“What do you think?” She pushed herself up and would have turned around except that he gripped her thighs and wouldn’t let her move. Then he spread her open and licked her clit and she trembled, another moan rising in her throat as he speared his tongue into her. “Cody!”

His name on her lips drove him. He licked and sucked her until she came again, and then he bent her over with her hands grasping the footboard and fucked her from behind until they were both mindless from the pleasure.

When it was over, they collapsed together and fell asleep entwined in each other's arms like two people who couldn't bear to be parted.

Two days passed in a haze of work and mind-blowing sex. Miranda got up each morning ready to do the duties of moving supplies and handing them out to the Jorwanis, who lined up each day looking for rice and milk and clean water. It was hard work, but gratifying. At night, when she was certain she couldn't move another muscle, she lay entwined with Cody, his cock buried deep inside her, their bodies moving in rhythm together, their tongues tangling with a desperation born of seeing so much suffering and agony.

Sometimes the sex was slow and thoroughly devastating to her senses, and other times it was hard and fast and raw. She rode him hard, demanding all he had to give, and then he'd flip her onto her back and show her exactly who was in control.

She was in love with his mouth. His beautiful, clever mouth that did things to her body she had never dared to dream could be so good. He seemed to have an obsession with licking her, and she didn't really mind. Because when Cody got his tongue on her, it was always earth-shattering. She got to lick him too, but not quite as often.

The first time she forced him to come while she gave him a blow job would be imprinted on her memory forever. He'd tried to stop her, but she'd refused to be moved. And then he'd stiffened and suddenly her throat was filled with him. It was almost too much, but she'd taken him completely. He'd collapsed afterward and hadn't moved for a long while. When he did, he'd kissed her soft and slow and told her that what she'd just done was amazing.

She figured he was just being nice, because Cody was the kind of guy who'd no doubt had a thousand blow jobs from willing women, and many of them more skilled than she—but she'd preened anyway. And then he'd pushed her onto her back and got his revenge by taking her to the edge again and again before he let her plunge over the side.

It sounded like a lot of sex, but it wasn't. Two hours a day, tops. Four hours in two days. Such a brief, intense affair—and quite possibly it would all end tomorrow when they went after Conti. Cody had said nothing about after, nothing about when they returned to DC.

And what could he say? She didn't even know where she'd be. If she'd have her life back and Sam would have found the mole, or if she'd still be on the run and looking for whoever had betrayed her. It was depressing to think about her life continuing the way it always had. She'd been driven, yes, and she worked hard at her job—but she'd been so lonely. She hadn't realized precisely how lonely until she'd met Cody.

From the first moment she'd known him, he'd been bigger than life. He commanded attention and he filled all the empty corners of her existence in ways she couldn't have predicted. She didn't want to need him in her life—but dammit, she liked having him there.

She looked up from where she was stacking boxes of supplies and caught his gaze across the courtyard. She felt those blue eyes like a flame burning into her. He jerked his head slightly and she took his meaning.

"I need a quick break," she said to Lucky. "Be back in a few."

"Yep," the other woman replied, not missing a beat.

Miranda headed into the building and made her way to the room she shared with Cody. He hadn't said where to go, but she knew. She was there first, and when the door opened and he walked in, her breath caught at the sight of him. He was tanned and sweaty, muscles glistening and teeth flashing white as he shut the door behind him.

He didn't have to say a word to her, and she was on him, throwing her arms around his neck, her mouth fusing with his, tongues tangling as he lifted her up and held her hard against him. She always felt like a delicate and precious thing when he wrapped his arms around her. Her heart beat fast, and she fancied that she could feel his beating equally fast against her.

"In you. Now," he said against her mouth, and she began ripping at his shorts while he shoved up the skirt of the cotton dress she wore and yanked her panties down. Another few moments and he was inside her, her legs wrapped around his waist, his hands supporting her ass, their bodies frantically straining toward the peak.

It didn't take long, and then he was setting her down on shaky legs, zipping his shorts and buttoning them again. Miranda cleaned up as best she could and slipped her panties on again. When she finished, Cody was watching her. He slid his fingers over her cheek, and her skin tingled along the path he took. The look in his eyes made her throat tighten.

She wanted to ask him what this was, what happened

after the mission was over, but her tongue wouldn't form the words. She'd built her life on not needing anyone. Admitting that she wanted more was tantamount to confessing a weakness. And if he rejected her? God, she didn't think she could take it.

"We better get back," he said, his eyes still fastened on hers.

She put her hand on his wrist, held it loosely. "Do you think they know?"

He snorted softly. "Probably. Do you mind?"

"No… but if I did?" Because she was curious what he would say then.

He put his other hand on her jaw, cupped her gently, thumbs sweeping along her cheekbones. "I'd hate that I put you in that position."

"I'm not delicate, Cody. I think you know that."

"The toughest woman I've ever run across. No lie."

It was her turn to snort. "Tougher than Lucky or Victoria? I doubt that."

"Tougher," he said, and she started to scoff but he put a thumb over her lips and stopped her. "Yeah, they're hard-assed and they get the job done. But I'm partial to you. You got the jump on me in Vegas, and trust me when I say that never happens."

Her breath hitched. Ridiculously, she wanted to cry. But only a little bit. The rest of her was standing strong against the emotion beating at the door. "I didn't get the jump on you. You could have disarmed me the instant you felt the gun—but you didn't because you were curious."

His brows drew down. And then he laughed. "How did you know?"

"I didn't at the time. I figured it out when you disarmed me after we got to the Rio. You could have taken me down in the Venetian, but you didn't."

He shrugged. "You looked like you needed a way out. And you were hot."

"Do you often let strange women hold you at gun-point just because they're hot?"

"Only once, baby. Only you."

She shivered at the way he said *only you*. "Maybe I should cuff you sometime. Tie you to the bed."

As soon as she said it, she wished she could call the words back. They implied a future—and he could shoot them down in a heartbeat.

His lids lowered, making him look hot and lazily sensual. "Maybe so. Or maybe I'll tie you up instead."

"I thought of it first."

"We'll just have to see who gets the jump on who, I guess."

His words gave her the confidence to say what she was thinking. "Does this mean we might see each other after we return to the States? Or do I need to find some handcuffs in Ian's storeroom and tie you up tonight?"

He let his hands slip to her shoulders. "Let's see what happens when we get back home."

It wasn't a promise, wasn't even an answer really, but she forced herself to smile anyway. "Sounds good."

"We better get back to work." He dropped his hands and turned to the door. When he opened it, Cash stood there, fist poised as if he was about to knock.

"Oh good, you're both here." He said it mildly, as if it was merely a statement of fact, but Miranda heard the hint of sarcasm beneath. He knew what was going on. They all did.

"What's up?" Cody asked as if this was the most normal circumstance in the world.

Cash's eyes flicked to her and then back. "Viking and Richie called a meeting. Conti's moving to the ship."

CHAPTER TWENTY-SEVEN

"I'LL DO IT," Miranda said, and everything inside Cody grew still. A moment later, anger flared inside him. She didn't look at him. He didn't expect she would. They'd left their room and come to Black's war room just a few minutes ago. Everyone had been straggling in, but when they were all there, Black announced that he had confirmation Conti was moving to the ship. Unfortunately he was flying, taking a helicopter from the presidential palace to the harbor, so there would be no waylaying him on the road.

And there'd only been more bad news. They didn't know where he would be located once he boarded the ship. They could storm it and search—or they could send in a prostitute with a tracking device. The instant that scenario was suggested, Cody had known where this was going.

"We can take Conti without her going in," Cody said, and everyone looked at him. They knew he was banging Miranda. It was evident on their faces. And that made him angry. Angry because he hadn't protected her more, hadn't protected their privacy.

Or maybe he just sucked at poker faces. He hadn't told anyone what was going on, but he hadn't needed to. Because it was obvious as hell, and that was his fault. *Shit.*

"It's faster this way, Cowboy," Viking said. "We shouldn't even be here, so the faster we get in and out, the better."

He didn't want to accept the truth of that statement, but what choice was there? Miranda was an agent, a trained operative. She wasn't some random woman they'd found on the street. She was accustomed to danger, and she knew how to handle herself.

Yet he hated the idea. He knew what it was like to lose her, even if that hadn't been real, but he thought if it happened again— Well, he wasn't going to enjoy it, that's for sure. His gut felt like there was a stone sitting solid and heavy right in the middle of it. He liked her, and he definitely liked having sex with her. He wanted more of the same for as long as it felt good.

He did not want her facing off with that douche bag Conti and trying to stave off a sexual assault while waiting for HOT to get there. Logically, he knew the likelihood of sexual assault was slim. Miranda wasn't going to allow it. And HOT wasn't going to fail to take the ship and extract the bad guy.

"When does she go in?" Viking asked Black.

"I'm waiting for the madam to contact me," Black said. He glanced at his watch. "If I had to guess, I'd say around nine tonight. That's about when he's asked for the other girls to show up each night."

"Six hours," Money said.

"And it's not dark for another five hours or so," Cody added. "We'll have to get into the water and over to the harbor fast."

"We'll make it," Viking said.

"I'm going to need much sluttier clothes than this," Miranda said, and Cody thought his jaw might crack from gritting his teeth.

"We'll find something," Victoria said.

"Exfiltration," Alpha Squad commander Matt "Richie Rich" Girard interjected. "We need to go over it again."

One of the IT guys pulled up a map on the computer screen overhead.

"Two vans waiting here," Black said.

"We're going to need to put our guys in charge of those vans," Viking drawled. "Or this is a no-go."

Black held up his hands. "Just trying to help. Fine, so you leave four guys with two vans. You still have fourteen operators—"

"Sixteen," Victoria said. "You forgot Lucky and me."

Ian Black gave her a look that wasn't precisely friendly but wasn't hateful either. Cody would have said there was a world of meaning in that look—and a long story too.

"Sixteen," he corrected. "My mistake."

"When you retrieve Conti, take him to the airport. There will be a plane waiting—but the window is tight, so you have to get there and get him on it."

"You realize we're going to need Colonel Mendez's authorization before we do that, right?" Nick Brandon said.

If Black had looked at Victoria with anything approximating unfriendliness, the look he gave Brandy was downright hostile. What had Lucky said on the plane? That there would be fireworks when the Brandons got in the same room as Ian Black?

Yep, the sparks were definitely flying now.

"I'm fully aware you need his permission to take a piss. Don't worry, I'll wait while you precious babies call and ask for his blessing."

"No offense, dude, but for all we know, you plan to get your hands on Conti and sell him to the highest bidder," Viking added.

Black shrugged. "I'd agree with your assessment except there's something else I want more." He didn't wait for them to ask what that was. "The ship and its contents."

Nobody said anything at first. They were probably all trying to figure out what Black's angle was.

"How the fuck are you going to steal an entire ship without anyone figuring out what's going on?" Cody asked.

Black's gaze was dark—and remarkably unconcerned. "The same way I do everything, SEAL. I'm going to pay the captain more than Conti was doing, and I'm going to offer him a deal he can't refuse."

"And what if the cargo is human?" Miranda demanded. She'd stood up to face Black, hands on hips, eyes flashing. She looked magnificently furious, and Cody felt his heart quicken. And other parts, which he managed to talk down before he embarrassed himself.

"If there are women on board, they won't be the only cargo. And they aren't what I'm looking for. They'll be returned to their families, should they want to go, or they'll be taken to refugee camps over the border where they'll be safe from Okonjo's schemes. I have no interest in human cargo other than to free them."

"Why should we believe you?" Miranda asked. "Women are valuable in the right places, and you want the cargo."

Ian Black snorted. "Been drinking the CIA Kool-Aid, darling? And how far has it gotten you?" He sliced a hand through the air, cutting off any debate. "I don't care if you believe me, Agent *Wood.* Your faith or lack of doesn't concern me in the slightest. I don't deal in human beings, end of story. If you'd like to rethink your participation in this mission, I'm sure the agency would welcome you back with open arms. I can put you in touch with someone who can get you home safe and sound."

Cody bristled at the man's tone, but Miranda's mouth only tightened. And then she tossed her hair. "No thanks. I'm not leaving."

"Didn't think so." Black spoke to the room in general. "Call your commander and brief him." He headed for the door and stopped just before he walked out. "Let me know when you're ready to move, pussies."

Lucky and Victoria had procured a short skirt and high heels from somewhere. They'd also produced a cut-off tank top that clung to Miranda's breasts and exposed her midriff. She looked at herself in the small sliver of mirror they'd brought to her room and wondered if Conti would recognize her and how long it might take if so.

She'd teased her hair and put on the makeup they'd given her. She used the green to highlight her eyes and hopefully throw Conti off. She also emphasized her mouth, making her lips fuller with liner and poutier with deep red lipstick. She had the same nose, of course, but there was nothing to be done about that.

She looked longingly at the 9 mil she'd taken from the weapons room, but there was nowhere to put it. Her clothes were too skimpy for a holster, and she wasn't going to be allowed a purse. She was going in with nothing but her personal-defense training and a bio-tracker device that she'd applied at the back of her neck beneath her hair. Not that those things wouldn't be enough, but a gun was always a nice touch when dealing with a sleazebag like Conti.

She finished everything and headed to the front of the compound. Conti had called, as predicted, and asked for a girl at nine thirty, which meant that HOT had a little more time to get into place. She didn't need to go anywhere just yet, but she wanted to see Cody. The teams were about to leave so they could slip into the harbor and prepare to infiltrate the ship.

When she emerged from the building, her gaze immediately went to him. He was standing with a couple of his teammates and they were clad in wetsuits. Her heart thumped at the sight of the man who rocked her world. The wetsuit clung to his form, showing off his incredible body to perfection. His dark hair was wild where the wind had whipped it up and toyed with it.

His blue eyes were like laser beams when he lifted his head and saw her. She could read everything in that gaze—anger, frustration, desire, regret. It made her shiver.

He said something to Cash and Alex Kamarov—she was getting better at knowing their names—and strolled toward her, all rippling muscle and lazy grace. His gaze raked her from head to toe as he came to a halt in front of her.

"Wow," he growled, and the pit in her belly hollowed even more at the sensual tone of his voice.

"Wow yourself," she said.

"You look hot, Miranda Jane." He pitched his voice low so no one else could hear even though they stood apart from the rest.

"So do you, Cody—wait, what's your middle name?" It occurred to her that she still knew so little about him. Knew so little and wanted to know so much. Wanted to know *everything.*

"Callum," he said, and she smiled.

"Cody Callum McCormick. That just trips off the tongue, doesn't it?"

He shrugged. "That's what Maggie thought."

"Maggie?"

"My mother."

The mother he'd told her was an alcoholic like her own. She still remembered how comfortable she'd been with him that night. Far more comfortable than she'd ever been with anyone else besides Mark—and that had taken months, not just a few hours like it had with Cody.

"It's also my grandfather's name—the Callum part, that is."

"Well, you look hot too, Cody Callum McCormick. I've never seen a man in a wetsuit before. It's very appealing."

"I'll let you peel me out of one after this is all over."

She grinned. "I'd like that."

His gaze darkened. "Be careful tonight. If Conti recognizes you… Well, it'll turn bad quickly if he does. As if trying to get under that tiny skirt isn't bad enough."

"I know what I'm doing. I won't take chances. I promise you that."

"You aren't planning a death scene, are you? Because I'd sure like to know it this time."

She smiled softly. "Not on purpose. And not if I can help it either."

He looked troubled. "That was a rotten trick, but I've been thinking about it, and I understand why you felt like you had to do it. But trust me when I tell you that you don't have to lie to me. I'll protect your secrets like they're my own."

"I know you will."

He took a step closer to her, wrapped an arm around her and tugged her in close in spite of their audience. "We're going to get Conti and we're gonna find who set you up. You'll get your life back. No more running or living in the shadows. No more target on your back."

Her throat was tight as she put her hands on his chest. She wanted to hold him tight and never let go. Such a strange feeling, but it was what it was. She was getting used to it. Maybe too used to it since she had no idea if he felt the same.

"I hope you're right. I'm tired of running—and tired of chasing."

"You mean Mark's killer?"

"Yes. I wanted justice for him—and I still do. But if I can't find who ordered him killed, then I'll live with that and know I did the best I could."

Cody squeezed her to him. It was meant to be a comforting hug, and yet it caused little explosions to go off inside her. Like always. Whenever this man touched her, she came alive in ways that were still surprising to her.

"Life is for the living, Miranda. It's not meant to be spent constantly engaged in the past."

"For a big brawny guy, you sure are smart."

He snorted. "Yeah, don't let the muscles fool you. There's a brain in here too."

"I want to kiss you," she said. "But I don't want to get this lipstick all over you."

"I don't fucking care about lipstick," he growled before crushing his mouth down on hers.

Vaguely, she heard hoots in the background. But that didn't stop Cody from kissing her senseless, or her from clinging to him like she wouldn't be able to stand on her own if he let her go.

"Gotta go, Cowboy!" someone yelled.

He broke away and stared down at her hotly. His mouth was red from the lipstick, but he still managed to look sexy as hell.

"You'd better wipe that off," she said, "or the guys will never let you live it down."

He dragged the back of his hand over his mouth and grinned when he looked at the color there. "You need to fix your mouth, honey. Somebody kissed off all your lipstick." He started walking backward, away from her.

"Take care of yourself, Cowboy," she said, her stomach churning as she thought about what he was getting ready to do. She wasn't frightened for herself, but if anything happened to Cody…

"You too, sunshine. I still need more."

She knew what he meant. "I do too."

He climbed into a waiting van along with the other SEALs and Alpha Squad. Then they roared into the street and sped away. Miranda's eyes stung as she watched them go.

"Be safe, Cody," she whispered.

CHAPTER TWENTY-EIGHT

MIRANDA WATCHED THE ship growing bigger as the car she was riding in sped toward it. The harbor lights shone on a dull red hull. The top of the ship was black and white. The lights illuminated men on deck too. She tried to count them but it was impossible to get an accurate number as the car got closer and the top deck disappeared from view. She'd lost track at five.

The ship wasn't the biggest one in the harbor, but it was still pretty big.

The driver stopped and turned to her. He pointed at the gangway leading into the side of the ship and spoke in broken English. "You go. They wait for you. When you done, Miss Dira send car."

Not that it mattered, but Miranda asked anyway. "How will she know I'm ready?"

"She send car in morning. You wait."

"And if Mr. Conti is finished with me at midnight?"

"You wait."

Miranda rolled her eyes as she climbed from the car. Yeah, not waiting. Not hardly. Ian Black had driven her to Miss Dira's brothel himself. She'd asked him point-blank why he was helping HOT if he'd been disavowed—and why they were accepting his help, even if they didn't accept it without some suspicion. *Trust but verify.*

He'd looked at her with that enigmatic gaze, and she'd known she wasn't going to get anything out of him. He was a brutally handsome man, the kind that made women of all ages swoon. But he did nothing for her. Nobody but Cody did these days.

"Have you ever played with one of those Chinese finger puzzles? You stick your fingers in and then you can't get them out, no matter how hard you pull?"

She shook her head. She knew what those were, of course, but she'd never played with one. And she didn't know what the hell that had to do with the question she'd just asked.

"I'm still pulling, Miranda," he'd said.

She hadn't even been surprised that he knew her name. At that point, she'd expected it. "Maybe you have to stop pulling then."

He'd grinned. "Yeah, well, maybe I will one of these days. Right now, I'm not ready to stop."

"I'm not sure I understand a damn thing you just said. But I get the point. You're stuck in something and there's no way out just yet."

"Maybe there is a way," he said. "Maybe I'm not willing to take it."

They'd arrived at the brothel then and a tall, dark-skinned woman walked out to greet them. Her name was Dira and she was gorgeous. She'd taken one look at Miranda and decided she was going to be a French hooker who'd just arrived in Jorwani. Miranda didn't bother to ask how she'd supposedly arrived, but she got the idea it wasn't completely willingly.

Disgusting thought, but there it was. Now she stepped up the gangway and walked onto the ship as a man motioned her forward. He gave her a rough pat-down, squeezing her ass as he did so. When he reached her breasts, she closed her eyes and gritted her teeth as he felt her up. She could elbow him in the stomach, whip around and knee his balls—but that wouldn't get her where she needed to go. So she endured the groping and then meekly followed along as he led her into the bowels of the ship.

It was a confusing warren of passages. She thought about Cody and his team trying to find her in this metal monstrosity, and she hoped to God the tracker device worked this deep in the ship. Lucky had told her that HOT might not get a signal from her until they were on board.

Miranda peered into dark corners and passageways as they walked, trying to get a hint about the cargo that Conti was so keen on—and that Black wanted.

But there was nothing she could see, nothing that indicated what was so important to either man. If there were women on this ship, they weren't being kept anywhere close to where she was headed.

They were still belowdecks when the man stopped at a door and rapped on it. A rough voice that she recognized told him to enter. He swung the door open to reveal a suite that looked like something from a cheesy porn set.

Dear God, Victor Conti was disgusting. The room was shadowed in pink light—a plus for her since it wouldn't illuminate her face too much—and incense permeated the air. Conti was lying back on a large bed with black satin sheets, the burgundy smoking jacket he wore barely concealing his formfitting black briefs. She decided that was done on purpose. He'd very clearly arranged himself in such a way as to show off his assets—or what he considered his assets.

Bile rose in her throat but she swallowed it down.

"You can go," he told the man, who bowed and walked out of the room, shutting the door behind him. At least it wasn't locked.

A fine sheen of sweat rose on Miranda's skin. It was disgust, pure and simple. But she had a role to play and she was going to play it. Because HOT was extracting this dirtbag tonight thanks to her willingness to stand here with a tracking device.

"What's your name?" Conti asked.

Miranda only smiled. She'd been told to pretend she didn't speak English. That worked for her.

Conti swore as he climbed to his feet. "Ah yes, Dira said you spoke no English. Fresh off the boat from France, she said. But she also said you'd know what to do."

He came over and walked around her very slowly, studying her. Then he reached out and took her chin between his fingers and turned her face this way and that.

Her heart pounded, but she worked to keep her face smooth and calm.

"Very pretty," he said. "Very pretty." He started to untie his robe. "I want to see that mouth wrapped around my dick, pretty girl."

Come on, Cody and the gang. Don't make me do this.

She grabbed for the tie of his robe and slipped it open. Conti's eyes gleamed. "Yes, baby, that's what I want."

But she didn't stop there. She made a game of it, pulling the sash all the way from the robe and holding on to it. She could tie him up with this thing. But how soon should she do it? If she disabled him now, what if HOT didn't show up for another hour? Fuck, she hated being out of the comm loop, but there'd been no way to keep her in it.

She just had to trust that they were coming.

The SEALs slipped into the Zodiac boats that would take them to the harbor. Cody slung his pack onto the floor in front of him and waited impatiently to be under way. Some of the Alpha Squad operators were coming with them and planned to split off to find the cargo while the SEALs secured the ship and went after Conti. Though SEALs were typically considered to be the combat swimmers, in reality all Special Operators went through combat-swim training—which meant the Army guys were perfectly capable of keeping up on this mission.

The rest of Alpha Squad would be waiting at the docks. The Brandons, both expert snipers, were on overwatch duty, tucked into a building overlooking Conti's ship. From there they could report on the number of men on deck as well as eliminate any threats that cropped up while the team was infiltrating the target.

The boats fired up and they motored off into the night. Cody could see the harbor lights up ahead, and he knew which ship was Conti's. The harbor wasn't that big, thankfully, and Conti's ship was docked in an area by itself.

The wind was cool on his face, but not cold. Jorwani was temperate for most of the year with both a rainy and a dry season. Fortunately, it was the dry season.

He thought of Miranda. Of that kiss. Hell, of every touch over the past couple of days. He'd been so fucking mad at her, and yet he'd wanted her too. He'd been determined to have nothing to do with her, and then he'd buckled at the first sign that Money might be trying to get into her panties.

No way in hell. That was *his* pussy. His mouth. His body. His, well, *everything*. He was learning to go with the flow of that idea, though he wasn't sure how long it would last. But right now, it showed no signs of going away anytime soon.

He tried not to think of the danger she was putting herself in tonight, but he couldn't quite block it out. The last time they'd faced off against a foe, she'd died. It hadn't been real, of course, but this time—hell, this time it was all real. The foe. The danger. The possibility that she could die. He wasn't going to be there to protect her from Conti, at least not for the first few minutes. What if the man recognized her?

He told himself that wasn't very likely. She had red hair. She had green eyes. She'd been wearing a shitload of makeup tonight that made her look different than usual. Conti would have to be damn good to notice she was the same woman in the little amount of time he was going to be with her.

But even if he did—fuck, Miranda was a professional. She could take down an assailant lightning fast. He didn't doubt her skills—but that didn't stop him from worrying.

The boats entered the mouth of the harbor and skirted along the edges, getting as close to the ship as they dared. They cut the engines, and then everyone slipped into the sea with their waterproof packs on their backs. They were each wearing a Rapid Diver system, which was attached to a harness and capable of providing them with twenty minutes or so of air without taking up the kind of space ordinary scuba equipment would. Twenty minutes would allow them to swim underwater to the ship and surface undetected.

When they reached the ship's fire line, Cody slipped out of the harness for the RDS and stowed it against the hull. Everyone else did the same. If they had to exfil by water, they could retrieve the devices and go. But the plan was that Ian Black's men would collect the devices when they took control of the ship.

Cody waited his turn to go up the fire line. He climbed hand over hand and slipped over the railing and onto the deck. Everyone got out their night vision and comm equipment. They inserted microphones and ear pieces and surveyed the area with their scopes. Next, weapons were removed from waterproof bags and everything stowed for their return.

"Brandy, we've reached the deck. Report," Viking said into the mic.

"Copy, Viking. Three male skinnies on aft deck, starboard. Smoking. How copy?"

"Viking copies all. We're going to put them to sleep and go below. You got a read on Juliet Whiskey?"

Juliet Whiskey—JW—was Miranda. Cody's heart thumped.

"Not since she went below. We're too far from the signal."

"All right. Viking out."

"Roger that, Viking. Good luck."

Viking shot a look at Blade, who was fiddling with his radio equipment. "Got her," Blade said. "Signal's faint, but it's enough."

They'd known this could be a problem with the steel hull deflecting the signal, but at least they had enough to go in and get her.

"Let's get the skinnies," Cage said. "Camel, with me."

The two of them ghosted away toward the aft deck, two others headed toward the bridge, and the rest of the SEALs started toward one of the metal doors that led into the ship's interior. If Conti expected invasion, he'd have had his men set up funnels and trip grenades to warn them of intruders. But nothing in the intel Ian Black had gotten indicated that Conti had reason to believe a team of American military Special Operators was on their way to get him.

Still, they would follow their training and slip through the passageways carefully, looking for trip wires and bolted doors that funneled them into a specific path where they might be ambushed.

And then, once they got through all that and found where Conti was trying to get his freak on with Miranda, they were going to take that motherfucker down and bring him to justice.

Cody only hoped they got there fast.

CHAPTER TWENTY-NINE

"EASY, BABY," VICTOR Conti said as Miranda slipped the sash around his neck playfully. She smiled when she did it, rubbed her breasts against his chest, and tried not to vomit at the evidence of his arousal. His hands slipped to her waist, his fingers skimming her bare midriff, and it was everything she could do not to knee him in the balls just yet.

"Take off everything but your panties," Victor told her. His grip on her tightened as she tried to step out of his embrace. She met his eyes, forced herself not to look as disgusted as she felt. And then he glided his hands up and grasped the edge of her top. She had a choice now. She could let him slide it over her head or she could stop him.

"This, off," he said, raising his voice in that way people did when they thought speaking louder would help someone who didn't understand the language magically comprehend what they were saying. "And this," he continued, sliding a finger to the waistband of her skirt.

She smiled as if she understood what he meant. She took a step back, both ends of the sash still in her hand. She could jerk him forward with that, knock him off-balance while aiming a knee at his head. She'd grab the back of his skull and slam him into her knee. If it didn't knock him out, it would certainly disorient him long enough for her to restrain him.

She tightened her grip on the sash—and there was a sudden rap on the door. It made her jump, and Victor swore. He jerked the sash from her hands and whipped it around his waist, tying the robe closed again.

Goddammit, she'd lost her advantage.

"This had better be good," he barked.

Miranda sashayed toward the bed, scoping out the room while Victor was occupied. The door opened and someone came in. She didn't look at him as she let her gaze slide over the room. Looking for possible weapons.

"We've got a potential problem," a voice began, and Miranda's insides turned to liquid. She spun before she could think about what she was doing, her gaze landing on the man who'd come into the room and stood there talking to Victor Conti.

Mark?

"We found water on the deck," he said.

"So?"

"Well, it hasn't rained," the man who could not be Mark Reed, but most certainly was, said. "And the only water is below us."

"Intruders? From the water?" Conti seemed genuinely confused.

Miranda was more so. How could Mark be standing here? How could he be *alive* and how could he be working with Victor Conti? Or *was* he working with Conti? Maybe he was on assignment too—

No, it wouldn't go down like that. Would it?

"Special Operators, Victor. A military team."

"Jesus Christ," Conti swore. "What about the fucking cargo? They want it, don't they?"

"Probably." Mark's gaze suddenly swung to her, and she realized she'd been moving toward his voice the whole time. Trying to get a better look. Trying to explain what her eyes said was true but her heart insisted could not be.

His brows drew down as he studied her. And then, before she could react, he whipped his gun from its holster and aimed it at her.

"Not another step," he growled.

"How?" she asked, her voice barely more than a whisper.

"Wait just a fucking minute," Victor demanded. "You speak English? Who the hell are you?"

"She's CIA. You've met her before—though she's supposed to be fucking dead."

Victor's head swung her way.

"Say hello, Miranda," Mark said. "And then you're going to have to tell me precisely how many operators there are and what the plan is."

Her entire body shook, but not from fear. From fury. She clenched her fists at her sides and wished like hell she could wrap her hands around his throat. Her eyes stung with tears, and her heart— Oh, her heart hurt like it had never hurt before. Which pissed her off even more because she knew, didn't she, just how treacherous people could be? She'd learned in four years at the CIA that nothing was ever quite what it seemed.

"I mourned you," she said, ignoring his command to say hello. "I loved you, admired you—and you did *this*? Why? Why are you here with—with this *asshole*?"

Victor growled and took a step toward her.

"Not yet," Mark grated. "We need her. She could be our ticket out of here." To her he said, "I guess we're both good at faking death. And whether you believe it or not, I was sorry you died."

Miranda laughed. It was a bitter sound. He hadn't really answered her, though she hadn't expected him to. "You aren't getting out of here, Mark. There are two teams—TWO—coming for you. They aren't going to quit, and they aren't backing down."

It didn't matter if she said it. He already knew she wasn't here alone. And maybe knowing there were two teams would give him pause. That was a lot of Special Operators, each and every one a deadly killing machine.

He cocked the pistol then, but she didn't flinch. Then he swore and dropped it to his side. He couldn't kill her, not yet, and they both knew it.

"Shoot her!" Victor shouted. "What the fuck are you waiting for?"

"If she's alive, we have a chance. Dead, they'll fucking kill us both."

Victor subsided, but he didn't look happy about it.

"Do you want to know who's coming?" she asked, feeling like she was sitting on a stick of dynamite that was about to explode. The adrenaline and fury pumping through her was potent. She felt like she could do anything—*anything*. But she was also smart enough to realize that she couldn't—or not yet anyway. But she could stall him.

Take your time. Keep talking. Wait for Cody.

Cody. Why did she think of Cody instead of HOT? It hit her that she thought of him because she had utter faith he would come and help her. He wouldn't let her down, not like everyone else in her life had—not like Mark clearly had. He would come and he would help her make this right.

"I imagine it's SEAL Team Six," Mark said. "Or Delta." He sounded bored.

Which meant she took great delight in telling him the truth. "Wrong. It's HOT."

He seemed to stiffen for a second. "Fucking hell." Then his eyes narrowed. "Are you wearing a device?"

"No."

"You're lying."

"Search me if you want. You won't find anything because there is nothing."

The bio-tracker was invisible, a thin slice of clear film that contained a transmitter and adhered to her skin. The transmitter was good for twenty-four hours, at which point it faded away.

"She was searched," Victor said. "Before she was brought in. There's nothing on her."

Mark lifted his head as if he were listening for something. Miranda strained to hear anything other than the sounds of the ship, but there was nothing.

He lifted the gun again, pointing it at her. "We're getting out of here. *Now.*"

"Juliet Whiskey is on the move."

Cody's gut twisted. "Where the fuck is she going?" he asked before anyone else could.

"Can't quite tell yet," Blade said. "Away from us though."

Viking spoke into his mic. "Brandy, did you copy?"

"Copy," Brandy said. "Nothing topside yet. We'll let you know."

"Thanks. Viking out. Richie, you any closer to that cargo?" he asked the Alpha Squad commander.

"About to blow the door," came the reply. "You need time?"

"Yeah. Ten mikes should do it."

"Copy. Ten mikes until we blow the door. Richie out."

Fucking hell. Ten minutes to find Miranda and stop Conti—and a whole lot of passageway left to navigate.

"We gotta move faster," Cody said.

Viking blew out a breath. "Yeah. But we can't fuck up and let them know we're coming either."

They fanned out and continued through the passageways, searching for trip wires and locked doors. But everything was clear. It didn't take an especially large staff to run a ship of this size, which was also good for them so long as they steered clear of the crew areas. Still, if they ran across anyone, they'd restrain them. Most of these people were hired sailors doing a job. There was no need to kill unless threatened.

"She's moving topside," Blade said.

"Fucking hell, there's a helicopter coming in for a landing." It was Brandy's voice over the mic. "Do you copy?"

"Viking copies."

"Richie copies."

Cody started moving toward the stairs as fast as he could go while still maintaining the perimeter.

"Disable the bird. Repeat, disable the bird." It was Richie's voice giving the order to shoot the helicopter. But Cody wasn't taking a chance. Neither was his team. They were all with him, ghosting through the ship and up the flights of stairs that would take them back to the top.

"Blowing the door, Viking," Richie said.

"Roger that," Viking replied.

It didn't matter if there was noise now. Conti was attempting to escape and taking Miranda with him. Cody swore under his breath even while he prayed she was okay. She had to be okay because she was moving—but son of a bitch he'd been right that Conti might figure out she was the same woman who'd come after him in Vegas.

He had to get to her before Conti did something. Cody bounded up the last few steps and stopped to listen. He could hear the helicopter's rotor beating the air—and then there was a ping and a whine and the motor sputtered.

"It's a hit," Brandy said over the mic.

Cody and Money went first, kicking the door open and clearing the area in front of them. The rest of the team followed. They moved across the deck toward the helicopter pad, guns aiming at the wounded bird and the people standing beside it.

A man threw his arm around Miranda and hauled her back against him, the barrel of his pistol wedged against her temple. Cody's blood turned to ice, but he didn't stop moving until he was there on the pad, gun aimed at the man's head.

There was another man on the pad. Victor Conti was wearing a robe that gaped open to reveal black briefs. He brandished a pistol as if he believed it would stop them, but there was no way he was a threat. The dude with Miranda was the threat.

Conti didn't have the pistol for long. Cody was aware of Money closing in—and then he was on top of Conti, disarming him and binding his wrists behind his back while Conti screamed insults and death threats.

"Shut the fuck up, asshole," Money shouted above the noise of the helicopter and the screams of Conti.

The dude holding Miranda backed them against the helicopter and waited for the attack. Every instinct Cody had told him to take the shot and eliminate this asshole. It was a shot any one of them could take blindfolded—but he didn't squeeze the trigger just yet. What if this guy was someone of value? Someone high up in Conti's organization they could use in a game of prisoner's dilemma?

Tell this dude that Conti had blamed him for everything and maybe he'd turn on his boss. It was a classic maneuver and one that worked more often than not.

The helicopter's motor sputtered and whined before dying suddenly. The rotors still whipped the air, but they were slowing.

"You can't win this one," Cody said to the man. "Best to put down the weapon and let her go."

"Not happening, Cody McCormick," the man said,

and Cody stiffened involuntarily. How the fuck did this guy know his name?

He heard Camel growl something under his breath.

Miranda's head was tilted back, the column of her throat exposed above where the man had an arm around her collarbone. She didn't look scared at all, which freaked him out just a little bit. Yeah, he knew she was an agent—but he expected more emotion out of her. Instead, she looked calm. A cold finger of dread tickled his spine as he remembered where he'd last seen her look so calm in the face of danger. That day in the desert. Right before she'd walked out in front of the truck and faked her own death.

"Jane," he growled at her, reminding himself to use her false identity. "What the fuck is going on here? Who is this guy?"

Miranda gazed at Cody in his sexy wetsuit, rifle slung over his chest and currently aimed in her direction, and felt numb. Mark's arm around her was tight. The gun at her temple was no longer cool to the touch, but warm where it made contact with her skin.

"Cody, meet Mark Reed." She spat his name. "Mentor, friend, ex-lover—traitor."

Mark's grip tightened for a second. When he spoke, his voice was pitched low so that only she could hear him. "I tried to keep you away from it all, but you wouldn't fucking stop searching for answers. I told Badger that sending you to infiltrate Conti's operations was a suicide mission—but it was out of my hands by then."

"I don't believe you," she spat. "Badger isn't involved in this."

"Who do you think told the agency you were dangerous? Obsessed with Conti? It couldn't have been me. I don't work there anymore."

His words were like poison darts landing in her ears—the truth of them pierced her and sank deep. Badger had betrayed her too. Badger, whom she'd always thought was her friend. But then she'd thought Mark was her friend, and look how that turned out.

Anger boiled in her veins. She was pissed and hurt and trembling with fury. It was almost too much to bear. Her two closest friends, if you could have called them that, in the agency—and they'd wanted to eliminate her. She'd been doing her job, nothing more—and they had sold out. For what?

Money, no doubt. It made her sick to think of it.

"You aren't getting out of this alive, Reed," Cody called out, and she could hear the utter fury in his voice. He sounded harder and harsher than she'd ever heard him. "I'll drop you if you force me to. Let her go and you can live."

Mark ducked his head behind hers, eliminating himself as a target. "How good are you, Cody? Think you can kill me before I kill her?"

Miranda closed her eyes, her heart heavy. She lived in a world of lies and deceit because that's what she had to do for the job. She *knew* there was no black and white, that everything was shades of gray—but she'd thought she'd known Mark and Badger. She thought she'd known what they were fighting for.

Turns out she hadn't known a thing. Mark had never cared for her the way she'd cared for him. He'd never cared about the things she cared about—or the things these dark and dangerous HOT men and women cared about.

When she'd gone after Conti, she'd wanted to honor Mark's memory and his fight for everything right. What a sham.

She didn't feel obligated to him anymore. The loyalty she'd once had was gone. Mark was a liar and a traitor. The worst kind of user. He was as selfish and useless as her parents. He'd been kind to her for his own purposes, no other reason. Certainly not because he was a decent human being.

"You tried to recruit me," she said as the truth hit her. "A year ago."

He snorted. "You just now figured that out?"

He'd been deep in the Conti operation then. It was one of the rare times when he'd met her to pass information. He'd looked so self-assured that day. And he'd asked her when he'd sat beside her at the bar if she'd ever just wanted to run away from it all. Start over and do something different. She'd shaken her head and sipped her club soda. "Do what? There's nothing as important as what I'm already doing."

He'd slipped the packet into her open computer bag and given her a weary smile. "I thought you might say that. *Hasta la vista*, baby."

He'd walked out, and she hadn't seen him again before the bombing that allegedly took his life.

Miranda knew what she had to do now—because she wasn't letting him kill her, and she wasn't letting him get away. Maybe Mark would anticipate her, but she had to take the chance anyway. Miranda fixed her gaze on Cody, rolling her eyes back toward Mark. Cody's brows lowered a fraction. She didn't know if that meant he understood or if he was telling her no.

But it didn't matter because she wasn't waiting another moment.

Mark's grip had loosened since he couldn't hold her as tightly when he had to stoop to hide his head behind hers. The maneuver had put distance between them. Not a lot, but enough.

It was now or never. She threw herself into action. She spun in his grip, grabbing his gun hand and shoving it away while dropping so she could remove her head from the target zone. He pulled the trigger and she felt the recoil of the weapon near her head. The bullet whistled past her ear as the blast deafened her.

She lunged for the gun but Mark dropped to the tarmac, taking her with him in a tangle. She landed beside him, her ears ringing as she grabbed for the weapon that had clattered from his grip. But there was no need. His gaze was empty, glassy, and there were two neat holes in his forehead—a double tap. She glanced up at the blood and brains spattering the helicopter's side and knew the back of his head did not look so neat.

Mark was dead. Really, truly dead this time. After everything that had happened, she didn't expect that to affect her—but it did. She felt a sob welling in her chest—and then she was dragged up and into a man's arms.

Cody had dropped to a sitting position on the tarmac beside her and held her tightly, his body smelling like saltwater and sweat and spent ammunition. She wrapped her arms around him and held on, letting the angry, despairing tears she'd been holding in flow down her cheeks. She was not a crier, dammit, but she couldn't seem to help it this time.

Her ears were still ringing, and she couldn't hear a thing Cody said, but she knew he was speaking because she could feel his lips moving against her ear.

She turned her head so she didn't have to look at Mark's lifeless body. One of the SEALs came over and said something to Cody. A moment later he was standing and lifting her with him. It took her a moment to realize he intended to carry her off the ship.

"I can walk," she protested.

"No." She couldn't hear the word, but she recognized it when it formed on his lips. She could have fought him—but she was tired of fighting. Tired of throwing herself at a wall and getting nowhere.

Miranda laid her cheek against his chest and let him carry her off the ship and away from this nightmare.

CHAPTER THIRTY

THE EXFILTRATION WAS uneventful. HOT climbed into two vans, their prisoner bound and gagged, and rocketed off toward the airport. Zain Okonjo had left for Kenya with his security force, so no response would be coming from that quarter. The men who'd been manning Conti's ship were hired sailors, not a part of his personal army, so their investment in defending him was minimal. The men who actually worked for Conti's organization were few in number and had been rounded up and handed over to Ian Black's people. Black's people were also taking care of Mark Reed's body.

"What was the cargo?" Money asked Kev. Because while the SEALs had been grabbing Conti and saving Miranda, Alpha Squad had gone after the cargo and turned it over to Black.

Kev looked grim. "Sarin and mustard gas shells, along with the usual guns and ammo you'd expect from an arms dealer. There were also about forty girls ranging from thirteen to twenty or so."

Lucky's face showed her fury over the situation. "Disgusting asshole," she said. "It's a good damn thing he's on the other van. I'd be tempted to relieve him of his balls."

"Holy shit," Camel said. "And we turned the chemical weapons over to Black?"

Viking blew out a breath. "What choice did we have? Can't leave it for Okonjo to reclaim."

Lucky's eyes flashed. "Ian won't use the gas, if that's what you're thinking. He won't sell it either. He'll make sure it gets destroyed. The man is an opportunist, not a monster. He'll also make sure those girls are taken care of and returned to their families, in case you were wondering."

Camel looked appropriately chastened. "All right, just asking."

"Mendez will be in touch with him, you can bet on that," Lucky added.

Cody sat across from them, shoulder to shoulder with Miranda. He'd wanted to keep holding her when they'd gotten in the van, but she'd climbed off his lap when he sat down and positioned herself beside him. She hadn't spoken a word.

His stomach churned with emotions he had to work hard to contain. It was a strange feeling to be so on edge. But he could still recall every second that Mark Reed had held a gun to her head. And then when she'd launched into action—

His heart would have stopped if he hadn't been trained to keep going in spite of whatever was happening around him. She'd scared the hell out of him though. He'd known what she was doing, but it had still been terrifying. She'd given him a signal, and then she'd given him that determined look she had, the one that said she wasn't done fighting, and he'd braced himself for anything. Her actions had given him a shot. There'd never been any question he was going to take it.

But not before Reed got off a round of his own. A round that had come perilously close to ending Miranda's life for real. It chilled him to the bone to even think of it.

"Are you okay, Jane?" Lucky asked.

Miranda lifted her head. "I… Yes, I'm okay. My ears are still ringing, but it's getting better."

"That's good."

Cody didn't say anything because he couldn't think of the right words. What was he going to say to her? She'd loved Mark at one time. She'd been on a quest to find his killer when Cody had met her.

Yes, Mark had betrayed her, but Cody had been the one to actually kill him. Logically, he knew that Miranda had given him the shot. But what if she couldn't reconcile it in her head?

Memories had a way of obscuring the truth. What if her memories of Mark as a man who had mentored her and cared for her took precedence in her mind? What if she tried to find reasons for why things weren't the way they'd seemed tonight? What if she regretted giving Cody the chance to take him down?

They reached the airport, going around to a private area where Black had bribed the gate guards to let them in. Once they were through the gates, the vans sped toward a jet sitting on the tarmac with the engines running.

The jet was painted with the logo of a cargo-shipping

company, but that's not what the jet was. It was a leased 737 with passenger seats and a cargo bay where the CIA moved shipments of whatever they wanted to get into a country. In the case of Jorwani, who knew? Weapons and supplies for Black, maybe?

In this case, they were moving an arms dealer/human trafficker to a place where he was going to be questioned and probably detained for the rest of his natural life. It was far too good a sentence for him, but it was out of Cody's hands. While he might like to personally castrate the asshole for buying and selling women—not to mention whatever evil he'd planned with the chemical weapons—that wasn't how HOT operated. And Cody was HOT through and through. He believed in their mandate and their methods, even if it was sometimes extra difficult not to dispense a little retribution.

They boarded the jet and Viking shoved Conti into a seat, strapping him in for the duration. The man snarled curses until someone shoved a wadded-up T-shirt from their pack into his mouth. If there was any justice, that T-shirt was sweaty and dirty.

The team flopped into their seats and breathed for the first time all night as the jet began to speed down the runway. Within seconds, they were airborne.

There were high fives and raucous laughter, but Cody had eyes only for Miranda. She was sitting by a window, her head turned toward the shade that was closed—they were all closed, in fact, as stealth was still important here. He wanted to reach for her hand, but he didn't. Instead, he sat there stewing in his own doubt.

It was about an hour into the flight when Miranda stirred. Her eyes were red-rimmed as she turned her head.

He hated that she was hurting. It was especially shocking since he'd never seen her this way before. She was usually so stoic. Tears were not part of Miranda's usual repertoire.

"You okay?" he asked, his voice gravelly from disuse.

"Not really," she said. "I can't quite believe what happened tonight."

"I'm sorry, sunshine. There was nothing I could do. I had to shoot to kill."

Her eyes widened for a moment, and he wished like hell she would take out those contacts. He wanted to see *her*, not some version of her that wasn't quite right.

"I know you did. It was the right choice."

His brows drew down. "You agree?"

"Of course I do." She reached out and squeezed his hand. "He would have killed me. You had no other option."

She pulled her hand back, and he felt its absence like she'd taken away a warm blanket on a cold winter night. Which was odd because his distinct impression of her right now was of something cold and brittle. She was distant, disengaged. Not the warm, passionate Miranda he'd made love to last night.

Made love?

He sat there with that thought spinning in his head, his brain churning like a turbine, and considered what those words meant. Were they just another description for getting naked and losing himself in her body the same as he would any other woman's? Or were they something more?

He'd stripped her frantically the last time, and then he'd taken her against a wall, driving them both to the peak of pleasure. But was there more to it than simply a release?

It hit him like a blow that yes, there was something more going on here. He cared about this woman. Cared to the point of not being able to imagine his life without her right now. He didn't know what that meant, but he knew it meant something important.

For the first time in a long time, he felt like he was floating on the currents of a strange kind of happiness. It was the same kind of happiness he'd felt as a kid, riding his horse at a flat-out gallop across a field. He'd felt wild, free, like anything was possible in those moments. It had seemed so, even if returning home and finding Maggie drunk off her ass and his grandparents tight-lipped had put an end to that notion every single time.

As if thinking about his childhood made it happen, the euphoria stopped and a chill slipped over him. What if Miranda didn't feel the same way? What if, now that they had Conti and knew that Mark Reed was a traitor, she wanted to move on? They didn't have to work together anymore. There was no reason to see each other unless they decided to.

He thought of her walking out of his life and felt strangely empty. And that made him angry because Cody McCormick didn't need anyone. He'd spent a lifetime making sure that was true. He was a nomad, a guy who didn't put down any roots and who could move on at the drop of a hat. His only ties were to his grandparents, who would be there for him until their dying day.

He couldn't count on that from anyone else. Not Maggie. Not even HOT or the Navy. If he stopped performing, they would remove him from their ranks.

He cared about Miranda, but he wouldn't let himself count on her. She was here now, but she could be gone tomorrow. He reached for her hand, gripped it firmly. Her fingers were like ice. She lifted her head and looked at him, a question in her gaze.

"I'm glad you're alive," he said fiercely.

She smiled, and his heart beat a little bit harder. "I am too. Thank you for saving me this time."

Miranda thought about a lot of things on the long flight back to DC. She thought about Mark and Badger, and she thought about Cody. He'd killed Mark. She examined that fact from every side, but there'd been no other way. When she'd thanked him for saving her, she'd meant it.

She'd spoken by phone to Sam Spencer back in DC, and she'd told Sam about Mark and Badger. Sam had gotten quiet for a moment, and Miranda had wondered if she was still there.

"Thank you," she'd finally said. "You've done a great service to the agency. Mr. Price will be arrested before we've finished this phone call."

Jeffrey Price was Badger's real name. It was shocking in a way to hear it said aloud. Only a handful of people would ever know the identity behind a code name. Except Badger was no longer a name that belonged to Jeffrey Price. He'd given up that right when he'd betrayed the agency.

"I did my job," Miranda had muttered.

She didn't feel like she'd done anyone a great service. She felt a little stunned, like someone who'd been told their house had burned down and there was nothing left. She knew she had to pick up the pieces and start again, but she didn't feel ready to do it just yet.

She'd finished the call and gone back to her seat. Cody had looked up when she walked toward him, but he hadn't asked any questions.

He was another enigma she couldn't solve. Her heart insisted on beating harder every time she saw him, but what good did that do her? He'd saved her life, but he hadn't professed his undying love—or even his undying desire.

Did she want him to? She feared that she did, and she feared it was a direct result of being rejected so soundly by Mark. Not rejected in a sexual way, but rejected in that he'd thought absolutely nothing of betraying her trust—or of killing her, because he damned sure hadn't thought anything of that.

She wanted to be desired for who she was, and she recognized that feeling was even stronger now. She wanted to be valued, not used. She wanted the desire for her to be real. She did not want to be someone's pleasurable pastime or a temporary booty call.

And because she wanted those things so desperately, she turned away from Cody and kept to herself. If she let herself lean against him, if she tried to kiss him or touch him, she felt as if she might crumble like stale bread if he didn't give her precisely the response she wanted.

She needed too much, and therefore she was determined to need *nothing.*

It was a long flight, made longer by her determination not to beg the man sitting beside her to show some affection. Yes, he'd held her hand, but for the past several hours he'd not touched her at all, save for their shoulders bumping from time to time.

They refueled in the air to save time, but it was still around fourteen interminable hours before the plane landed at Joint Base Andrews. Ordinarily they'd have come into a commercial airport, but their cargo was too volatile to risk being seen by eyes that weren't carefully controlled.

Sam Spencer and Colonel Mendez were waiting when they stepped off the jet. Miranda fixed her gaze on them. Sam was so cool and contained, her blond hair shining in the runway lights. It was a chilly evening and she wore a trench coat. Perfect for a spy. She looked as if she was about to pass a classified briefcase to someone and then stride off into the night.

Colonel Mendez was something else altogether. Tall, dressed in ACUs, his jaw hard beneath lowered brows, he looked intense. Not that Miranda had ever seen him look any other way. If he had another setting, she didn't know it.

"Good job," he said as HOT stopped on the tarmac and saluted him. They weren't in uniform and they looked a bit worse for wear, but they were still a proud military outfit who revered their commander.

He returned the salute and everyone relaxed marginally.

"Cargo is safe and sound and ready to be off-loaded," Viking said, and Mendez nodded before turning to Sam and giving her a signal.

She motioned to two agents standing behind her, and they headed toward the plane to retrieve Victor Conti.

"Thank you," she said to the group when her agents were on their way up the stairs to the aircraft. "You've saved many lives and spared much pain in the world by bringing Conti back. He's a drop in the bucket, but one drop is a step forward in this fight."

She turned her head and speared Miranda with a look. "Agent Wood, with me please." She motioned toward a waiting car and Miranda nodded. She wanted desperately to look at Cody before she went, but she couldn't manage it. Instead, she walked behind Sam like an automaton and climbed inside the Cadillac.

When she was seated, she looked back at the group on the tarmac. They were moving around, gathering their bags and equipment.

But Cody stood stock-still, staring at her. Her belly clenched tight. She wanted him so much. Wanted to lose herself in his arms and kiss him hard and long before falling into bed with him and not coming up for air for days.

But it wasn't to be. The mission was over, and so was their affair. He wanted her body but he didn't want her heart. And that was no longer enough for her. If she'd learned nothing else on this mission, she'd learned that much. She was tired of being a pit stop on the road when what she really wanted was to be someone's destination. It wouldn't be easy with her job, but nothing worth having ever was.

She turned her head and stared straight ahead as the driver accelerated toward the main road. It was over. And it hurt far more than she'd ever thought possible.

CHAPTER THIRTY-ONE

CODY WAITED EXACTLY one week before he requested to see Colonel Mendez. He stood in the secretary's office in his ACUs with the Navy rank and insignia sewn onto the Army camouflage and waited for the skipper to see him or tell him to go away.

To his surprise, he was shown into the large office with the wood paneling and the photos of the skipper with various important government officials hanging on the wall.

"What can I help you with, Petty Officer?"

Cody stood at attention. The skipper—colonel—sat at his desk looking relaxed and curious at the same time.

"Sir, I was wondering about Agent Wood."

Mendez lifted an eyebrow. "What about her, Cowboy?"

Cody swallowed. Goddammit, this was the part where he'd known he would get tripped up. But when Miranda had walked away from him on the tarmac at Andrews, he'd realized that he didn't know where to find her. He could look her up—and he'd done so—but she was CIA. Like him, she wasn't easy to find. There was no Miranda Lockwood in DC. There were a few Jane Woods, but none of them were his Jane. He'd found the Lockwood family in Alabama, but he knew she didn't ever go back, so he hadn't tried to contact anyone there.

He would if he had to, but his first thought was the skipper. If Mendez didn't tell him what he wanted to know, he'd go to Alabama.

"I want to talk to her, sir."

Mendez sat back and folded his hands over his middle. "Then call her. I don't care if you do."

"Sir." Cody drew in a breath. "I don't have her number, sir."

Mendez actually snorted. "Jesus Christ, not much of an operator, are you?"

Cody would have been insulted except he could tell the skipper was ribbing him. Operator as in smooth, not special.

"No sir, not very smooth. I didn't get her number."

"What if she doesn't want to hear from you, son?"

Cody clenched his jaw. Yeah, that was possible. Maybe even probable considering she hadn't given him her number before she'd walked away.

"I'd like to give her the chance to tell me that herself, sir."

Mendez chuckled this time. "All right, sailor. I'll see what I can do." He shook his head. "You boys and your goddamn dicks. Pussy is freely available for men like you—and what do you do? Get hung up on one woman. Wrapped around her pretty little finger so hard you can't think about anything but her."

Cody felt himself going red. Was he hung up on Miranda? Yeah, he totally was. One week without her and he was slowly losing his mind. He didn't understand it, but he knew he had to see her again. "Yes, sir."

Because what else did you say to an O-6?

Mendez sighed. "Back to work, son. If I find anything, you'll know about it."

Miranda felt unmoored. There was something very life-changing about having two people you'd thought were your friends turn out to be traitors to everything you believed in.

She went about her life. She drove to the agency every day, and she sat in on briefings and did paperwork. Her return from the dead surprised no one. Not because they'd thought she was still alive, but simply because in the CIA you accepted that nothing was as it seemed.

Badger was arrested. She'd seen him through the two-way glass in the interrogation room. He'd snarled and cursed and looked like a different man than she'd known. Gone was the kind, solicitous, seemingly harmless handler who appeared to care about her. In his place was a hard, cold, dangerous man who had no love for his government or those in charge of the agency. He believed the way to American superiority in the world was far more violent than she did, and he was willing to use any means to get it.

Listening to him had shaken her up a bit. She wasn't ready to quit the agency or anything like that, but she was angry that someone she'd liked could be so twisted and horrible. She'd gone home that night and called her sister. Sherri was happy to hear from her, but also distracted in that way she always was because of kids and a husband.

"How's Mama and Daddy?" Miranda had asked after a while.

She could practically hear Sherri take the phone from her ear and gape at it. Miranda never asked about their parents.

"Mama's the same as always—drunk off her ass and killing herself with the liquor even though she denies it. But Daddy's found Jesus and he's cleaned up his ways. No more drinking or smoking. No more bar hopping. He goes to Bible study and he's joined the choir."

Miranda's jaw had dropped open. She'd snapped it closed and asked her sister about everyone else. By the time the call was over, she'd promised to come visit for a few days in the summer. And she felt surprisingly okay about it. In her experience, family wasn't a magical entity that loved you no matter what, but they were the people who had the most reason to. Maybe it was time to try to forge a relationship with some of them and see what happened.

She thought of Cody almost every minute of the day. She could still see him watching her as she'd driven away, his legs parted in a wide stance, his jaw hard, his brows drawn low. If he'd made even one move toward her, given her one gesture to come back to him, she'd have rocketed out of that car and flung herself in his arms.

She missed him like crazy. She craved him, and she

wasn't getting her fix, and that made her sad and angry and hopeless in ways she had never experienced before. She knew her feelings were out of whack, all wrapped up in Mark and Badger's betrayal and looking for a safe harbor in Cody.

She ached, but would she ache under other circumstances?

She was pretty sure the answer was no, so she made no move to seek him out. But she often thought of driving to that military base and standing outside the compound, in the parking lot, and waiting for him to emerge. She imagined his face, imagined that he would smile and then come over and take her in his arms.

She went even further than that. She imagined him picking her up and spinning her around while telling her that he loved her madly. It was a lovely fantasy, but it was just that: a fantasy.

At the end of yet another day at work, she turned off her computer and shouldered her purse, then drove home through rush-hour traffic, feeling lonely and cranky and completely out of sorts. What was wrong with her? She never stayed down long, but this time she felt like she'd never get back up again.

She stopped at her favorite guilty pleasure restaurant and picked up a pizza with extra cheese and pepperoni, which she planned to gorge on while sitting in front of the television and watching reruns of *The Big Bang Theory* because it made her laugh and she needed to laugh right now.

She parked in her spot, grabbed the pizza, and headed for her apartment on the second floor of the complex. When she reached the landing, she stopped, her heart leaping into her throat for a second.

A man sat on the floor, leaning back against the wall—and when he looked up at her, familiar blue eyes bored into hers. Her heart beat to its own crazy, reckless rhythm, hammering away in her chest like a mad thing while she tried to maintain some semblance of normalcy.

"Hi," he said, pushing to a standing position. He was wearing camouflage. The tape over his heart said U.S. Navy. The SEAL trident was above it. The tape over his right pectoral said McCormick. There was an American flag on his right shoulder and other patches that she didn't know the meaning of.

She took all that in very quickly, and then she was at a loss for what to say. Her brain kicked her mouth into gear with the thought that repeating the greeting was an appropriate response.

"Hi."

He nodded to the pizza in her hands. "Expecting company?"

It was a large pizza, which was silly, but when you were trying to forget about a man, you did silly things. "Nope. All for me."

He snorted and grinned. "Good for you, Miranda Jane. I like a woman with an appetite."

She handed him the pizza, because she couldn't think what else to do, and then inserted her key into the lock. When the door opened, she hesitated for a second. Then she turned to him and took the pizza.

"Why are you here?" she asked, standing in the doorframe and effectively blocking entrance to her home.

His eyes crinkled at the corners. "I told you it wasn't enough."

Her blood quickened. That's what she'd said to him back in Jorwani—that it wasn't enough, that she still wanted more.

And she did want more. Even now, standing there with him looking so hot and beautiful, she wanted to strip him of that panty-melting camo and have her wicked way with him. Repeatedly.

"I..."

She couldn't think of a thing to say. He took the pizza, gently, and pushed her backward. She stepped back willingly and he closed the door behind them. Then he set the pizza on the hall table and stepped up to her, cupping her face in his hands. His touch was so gentle, so necessary, that she whimpered.

"I missed you, Miranda," he said, his voice soft and deep. "I need you."

And then he kissed her, his mouth taking hers in a surprisingly gentle kiss. But it was still hot, still stoked the fires deep within her, still made her willing to do anything to have him fan those flames higher.

It hit her, suddenly and forcefully, that what she felt for this man was so much more than she'd ever felt for anyone else in her life. She'd thought she'd loved Mark at one time, but that had been a youthful infatuation kept aloft by what she'd perceived as his perfection. He hadn't been perfect at all—and he certainly hadn't loved her. He'd helped her, mentored her, but it had never been anything he'd had to make sacrifices to do. She could see now, thinking back on it, his selfishness and unwillingness to compromise.

Cody wasn't perfect. Cody didn't pretend to be perfect. He was strong and stubborn and arrogant and pushy when he wanted something. He was also loyal—to a cause, to his profession, to the people he worked with. He was the best that this nation had to offer in defense of its ideals, and he would die upholding those ideals if necessary.

And she would die if he walked out when he was finished with the sexual heat between them. Because she was in love with him. Stone-cold in love with a man she barely knew but felt like she'd known forever.

She put her hands on his wrists, tugged until he broke the kiss and let go. He looked confused and concerned, and she took the opportunity to step away from him.

"What's wrong, Miranda?"

She turned her back to him and took several deep breaths. She had to get herself under control. Had to face him with strength and determination, not fear or weakness.

He was waiting when she turned around again, his hands at his sides, fingers clenched into fists.

"I can't do this," she said, her voice sounding scratchy and hoarse. "I just can't."

"Do what?"

She waved a hand wildly, the beginning of the end of her control. "This! You. Me. Kissing you and losing my mind while you take me to bed. Wanting more than I should but being unable to stop."

"You're not making any sense," he growled. "What's wrong with losing your mind or wanting more? It's the same for me."

She choked back a sob. "No," she yelled at him. "It's *not* the same! You don't love me—you just want to fuck me until you're ready to move on to the next girl you meet!"

She sounded insane, she knew it, but she didn't care.

It was as if all the wild emotion she'd been holding in for so long was bubbling over and spilling out. She couldn't stop it. Couldn't hold it in.

"I can't do this because I want more," she said. "And not more sex. More *you*, Cody. More us, but us with a future. I want to know this is more than physical. I want someone to want the same things I do for a change. I want someone to want *me*."

She thought that would be it. The moment when he'd turn and walk out and she'd never see him again. She'd let it all spill out. She'd done everything but speak the words. Unless he was an idiot, he had to know that she'd fallen for him.

But he didn't walk out. He strode toward her, took her by the shoulders, and then dipped a finger under her chin and forced her to look up and into those beautiful blue eyes.

"There is no next girl. There's only you. There's only been you since I met you in Vegas. I don't know why, I damn sure don't know how, but you're in my soul, Miranda. You're so deep in there that all I can do is figure out how to be with you as much as possible. If I have to beg to be in your life, I'll do it. Hell, I went and begged my skipper to find you for me so I could see you again."

Her throat went dry. She was in his soul?

"I don't know what that means, Cody."

He looked troubled for a second. "It means that I suck at this, apparently. I'm not good with flowery words or speeches about feelings. Hell, I've never had to give them before—never wanted to. But you—God, Miranda—you make me want things I didn't think were possible. I'd say I love you, but I don't think it's enough—"

She put a hand over his mouth, her head spinning with happiness—and fear that she'd misunderstood him. "Why isn't it enough? It's what I want to hear. It's the only thing I want from you."

She lifted her hand slowly and he smiled.

"I love you, Miranda Jane Lockwood."

She let out a shaky sigh. Her knees were surprisingly weak, and her body trembled. "I love you too, Cody Callum McCormick."

He blinked. "You do?"

"I do."

He grabbed her around the waist and picked her up, hugging her tight. He didn't spin, but she didn't care. It was still her fantasy come true.

"You have no idea how much I want…" He waggled his eyebrows. "…that pizza," he finished, and she burst out laughing.

"That's *my* pizza, bucko."

"Can't you share with the man you love?" he asked, setting her down but not letting her go, his hands loosely holding her hips.

She reached up and ran her fingers over his cheek. He was hers. Truly hers. What an amazing feeling that was. So amazing she could hardly believe it was real just yet.

"You can have anything of mine you want."

He tugged her in close and bent to put his forehead on hers. "First, pizza. Then you for dessert."

"Sounds like a plan to me."

CHAPTER THIRTY-TWO

"DID HE SAY why he did it?" Cody asked. He was lying in Miranda's bed, his energy sapped after a very vigorous romp in the sheets. She was in his arms, gloriously naked, her body still flushed and damp from exertion.

They'd eaten the pizza while watching TV. He'd been happy to sit there with his arm around her and just enjoy being together. In fact, he'd fallen asleep on her couch with her tucked in beside him. She'd shaken him awake an hour or so later and told him he could stay the night if he wanted.

And he did want, but he didn't want to sleep. He'd stripped her slowly, kissing every inch of her as he went. And then he'd pushed her back on the bed and spread her legs, touched his tongue to the heart of her, and didn't stop until she was quivering and crying out.

When he'd finally entered her body, he'd shuddered with the force of the emotion he felt. It was different to be inside her and know he loved her, that her happiness and her pleasure were all he wanted. It heightened the sensations for him—and he'd come much faster than he'd wanted to. But that's okay, because he was already thinking about round two.

Miranda stirred against him. "He's a bitter, deluded man who thinks America has gotten too wrapped up in political correctness. We're soft on terrorism, immigration, and we allow sexual deviants to get married—his words, not mine. According to him, Conti had the money and the connections to get things done—eliminate the people who needed eliminating—Americans in government or on the bench who would then be replaced with the kind of people who wouldn't hesitate to take the fight to ISIS or the Freedom Force. Not to mention abolishing gay marriage and everything else he considers wrong with this country."

"Damn," Cody said. "I can understand having a strong political view, but advocating subversion and violence to achieve your objectives is definitely not the right thing to do. It's not what this country stands for—or what we fight for."

"Exactly. Badger—Jeff—knew Victor Conti from an old mission twenty years ago in which the agency actually worked with Conti instead of against him. He admired him—and he talked Mark into working with him to undermine the case against Conti. That's all it was supposed to be, but then Conti decided he wanted Mark to play a bigger role in his operations. So they faked his death, against Jeff's wishes, and then Jeff was put into a more subordinate role than he liked. Not to mention I don't think that Conti ever really shared his views—for him, it was about the inside connection in the CIA."

"And when you wanted to be the one to go after Conti, Badger encouraged it. Knowing you would have to be killed if you got too close."

He felt her stiffen for just a second, and he hated that someone'd had the power to hurt her like that.

"I'm not sure he thought I'd stay in it until the bitter end," she said. "I think he expected I'd lose heart—but support for the mission grew inside the agency, and I didn't quit. He thought he could control me, but he couldn't."

She tucked her hair behind her ears. It was still red, but she wasn't wearing the green contacts anymore. He'd asked her about the hair and she'd teased him at first, saying she was planning to keep it. He'd said that was fine, because what else could he say? It was her hair.

But she'd slapped him playfully and told him she had an appointment at the salon to return it to her natural color. Now she looked at him with those whiskey eyes, and his heart thumped a bit faster.

"They let you get close."

"They had to. If they'd sabotaged it any other way, they might have tipped their hand."

"I'm sorry, Miranda."

"It's not your fault."

"They hurt you. And I only killed one of them. If I could get the other, I'd gladly do it."

She laughed softly. "Just knowing you want to is enough, believe me."

He skimmed his fingers up and down her spine. He didn't miss the way she shivered or the way her eyes dilated with need.

"I was worried you blamed me for killing Mark. I know he meant something to you."

She sighed. "You had no choice. I know that. I don't blame you—and I'd have done the same damn thing if he'd been threatening you." She heaved herself up and planted a kiss on his mouth. It wasn't meant to be a sexy kiss, he didn't think, but of course it got out of control and ended up that way.

He rolled her to her back, their tongues gliding together as he kissed her deeply. She moaned and he pressed kisses to her jaw, her neck, as her arms twined around his back.

"I was also going to say," she gasped out, "that whatever he meant to me was a lie."

Cody worked his way to her breasts, sucked a beautiful nipple in his mouth, and tugged on it while her fingers curled into his shoulders.

"This isn't a lie," he told her, moving to the other breast. "This is real."

"Yes," she moaned as he took her nipple between his lips. "Yes…"

He loved her with everything he had, taking her to the peak again and again, her moans fueling him.

And then he was deep inside her again, his cock buried to the hilt, his entire body on fire with need and hope and belonging. They moved together like they were made for each other, bodies rising and falling and taking and giving.

Miranda shattered around him, his name a hoarse cry on her lips. He followed her over the edge, his body pouring itself into hers the same as he'd poured all his emotion into loving her.

"This is forever," he told her as he gazed down into her eyes. Beautiful, whiskey eyes.

She smiled and his heart swelled. "Yes," she whispered. "It is."

One month later…

THE CROWD AT Matt and Evie Girard's place was having a good time that night. Cash sat in one of the comfortable lawn chairs situated near the pool as his teammates played a wicked game of water polo. He'd been in the pool for a while, but now he wanted to kick back, observe the others, and catch up on some reading. He picked up his phone and scrolled through the newsfeed. Predictably depressing.

He let his gaze slide over the gathering. Matt and Evie's twin baby boys were kicking up a storm in their little bouncy chairs. Evie was busy feeding them some sort of pureed mush while she chatted with some of the other women gathered around. Cash didn't know them all, not yet, but he knew they were wives or girlfriends of Alpha Squad.

And then there were the women with the SEALs. Ivy Erikson and Christina Marchand sat together, chatting about God knows what. Babies probably, though Cash didn't know what made babies so interesting. They cried and crapped and threw up a lot—and they didn't let you sleep. Not his kind of thing at all.

There were also a couple of dates present—Camel had brought a woman with fake tits and bleached-blond hair. Not that those things were bad, because Cash loved that combination himself, but the frosted pink lipstick did her no favors, nor did the perpetually turned-down frown she sported.

The other woman was with Blade. She was a brunette with long legs and a great laugh who, upon being dunked in the pool, retaliated by doling out surprise wedgies. A much better addition to the group than Miss Sour Lips.

A cheer went up from the crowd just then, and Cash slewed his gaze toward the patio doors. Cowboy stood there with his hand entwined with his sexy CIA agent's. Miranda Lockwood was a gorgeous woman, that was for sure. He'd thought she was beautiful as a redhead—but with blond hair and golden eyes, she was a stunner.

Lucky fucking Cowboy. He'd come back to work a few weeks ago and announced that he was in love with Miranda and they were in a relationship. Could have blown Cash over with a puff of air. He'd known that Cowboy was hung up on her when they'd gone on the mission to grab Conti, but he hadn't known it was that serious.

Jesus. Love. How did a guy even know when that's what it was? Cowboy had only been fucking Miranda for a few days when he'd decided she was the one for him. How the hell did that happen?

Cash shook his head. No way that was happening to him. He loved women—and pussy—too much to ever limit himself to one for life. The world was a buffet, and he was happy sampling from it.

Cowboy stood there with his woman until she stood on tiptoe to kiss him and then went over to sit with Ivy and

Christina. Cash watched his teammate watching her and shook his head.

Dude's fucking balls were in her purse. He didn't move until she looked up and gave him a little wave. Then he strolled over to where Cash was and flopped back in a lounger.

"You look smug," Cash said, and Cowboy snorted before turning his gaze on him.

"Not smug. Happy. Content."

Cash snorted and took a sip of the Jack Daniel's Single Barrel he'd poured for himself. "Pussy whipped."

Cowboy merely grinned at him. "You can't piss me off, Money. I've got the woman of my dreams and life is good. Tease me all you want, but tonight when this shindig is over, I'm leaving here with the most gorgeous woman you've ever seen in your life. And she's mine, man. All mine."

Cash lifted his glass, feeling a little jealous even while he told himself that no way in fucking hell did he want to be as whipped as Cowboy.

"To you then."

Cowboy picked up the can of soda he'd carried over. "And to you. May you find the woman of your dreams and be as happy as I am."

"Not happening, dude. The woman of my dreams is *all* of them. How can I eat prime rib for the rest of my life when there's a delicious lobster waiting? Or a juicy hamburger?" He shook his head. "Nope, not me."

Cowboy laughed. "I'm going to remind you of this conversation someday. And I'm going to laugh my ass off when I do."

Cash shrugged. "It's a losing proposition, but whatever makes you happy."

Cowboy turned his head to gaze over at Miranda. She sent him a private smile, and Cash looked away, feeling like he was intruding on something.

"Miranda does," Cowboy said softly.

For the first time he could ever remember, Cash felt something very like jealousy blossom deep inside his soul. He took a sip of his drink, then lay back and closed his eyes. The feeling would pass, certainly. But for now, it made him feel hollow inside.

And that was a feeling he didn't like at all.

ABOUT THE AUTHOR

LYNN RAYE HARRIS is the *New York Times* and *USA Today* bestselling author of the HOSTILE OPERATIONS TEAM SERIES of military romances as well as 20 books for Harlequin Presents. A former finalist for the Romance Writers of America's Golden Heart Award and the National Readers Choice Award, Lynn lives in Alabama with her handsome former-military husband, two crazy cats, and one spoiled American Saddlebred horse. Lynn's books have been called "exceptional and emotional," "intense," and "sizzling." Lynn's books have sold over 3 million copies worldwide.

Connect with me online:
Facebook: https://www.facebook.com/AuthorLynnRayeHarris
Twitter: https://twitter.com/LynnRayeHarris
Website: http://www.LynnRayeHarris.com
Newsletter: http://bit.ly/LRHNews
Email: Lynn@LynnRayeHarris.com

Join my Hostile Operations Team Readers and Fans Group on Facebook:
https://www.facebook.com/groups/HOTReadersAndFans/

17914690R00162

Printed in Poland
by Amazon Fulfillment
Poland Sp. z o.o., Wrocław